Kid Pirates

Their Battles,
Shipwrecks,
& Narrow Escapes

TEN TRUE TALES

Kid Pirates

Their Battles,
Shipwrecks,
& Narrow Escapes

Allan Zullo

SCHOLASTIC INC.
New York   Toronto   London   Auckland   Sydney
Mexico City   New Delhi   Hong Kong   Buenos Aires

Photo Credits:
Skull: Corbis; Bones: Emma Lee/Life File/Photodisc/Getty Images

ISBN-13: 978-0-439-91813-8
ISBN-10: 0-439-91813-8

12 11 10 9   12 /0

Printed in the U.S.A.
First Scholastic printing, September 2007

To Danny "D" Manausa, who, if he had been born four centuries earlier, would have made a great pirate hunter.

— A. Z.

Contents

Kid Pirates

Their Battles,
Shipwrecks,
& Narrow Escapes

PIRATE SCUTTLEBUTT

When you think of pirates, you probably imagine the fun-loving, carefree, dashing swashbucklers portrayed in movies and novels — you know, the daring sea rovers who dived into one wild, breathtaking escapade after another just for the thrill of it.

But here's the truth: In real life, most pirates weren't nice people looking for adventure. They were brutal cutthroats who attacked and plundered ships, mostly out of sheer greed.

Pirates lived under horrible conditions — cramped quarters, lousy food, foul water — and regularly stared death in the face from vicious storms, sea battles, or tropical diseases. And even if they survived all those dangers, they knew that if they were ever captured, they faced the hangman's noose. That's because while pirates were hunting their prey, navies were hunting *them*. No wonder few pirates reached a ripe old age.

Yet they were willing to risk their lives for the chance to strike it rich.

From the late 1600s to the early 1800s, piracy thrived in the Caribbean Sea, Gulf of Mexico, Atlantic, and Indian oceans. Pirate ships were manned by a variety of seamen: penniless, desperate sailors who once served on merchant vessels and warships . . . cold-blooded thugs who were mad at the world . . . crewmen who were forced to join at gunpoint, or who chose to join after pirates had captured their ship.

And some pirates were *kids*.

This book features ten true stories about the perilous experiences of real-life young people who turned pirate either by choice or circumstance. They came from different backgrounds — such as the former slave, the wealthy heir, and the poor worker. Some embraced the pirate life; others hated it. Some were brought to trial; others escaped scot-free. Some fought as buccaneers (which is what pirates of the Caribbean Sea were called); others served as privateers (pirates licensed by a government to attack and plunder vessels from enemy countries).

These true stories — based on old memoirs, diaries, news accounts, personal journals, and court records — use real names, dates, and places, although the dialogue has been re-created and certain scenes dramatized. In the following pages, you will read about kids who served under notorious pirates such as Blackbeard, Captain Kidd, and Black Sam Bellamy.

Whether their consciences were clear or their hearts were bad, one thing is not in dispute. These kid pirates lived hair-raising lives.

— Allan Zullo

ESCAPE FROM MARACAIBO

DAVID CORNWALL,
SEAMAN FOR PRIVATEER HENRY MORGAN

Thrashing his arms and legs, David Cornwall howled, "Let me free! For God's sake, let me go! I can't take this torture anymore!"

"Hey," came an annoyed voice in the darkness. "Shut up, will you. Take your nightmares up on the deck and let the rest of us seadogs get some sleep."

David jerked awake and slipped out of his hammock in the ship's crowded living quarters. He was soaked in sweat and breathing heavily. *Another bad dream*, he told himself. *When will they end?*

The 15-year-old had been suffering from nightmares of his six months chained in a dungeon of unspeakable filth. Two years earlier, during a voyage from his native England, David, his parents, and 10 others were captured by Spanish pirates in the western Caribbean and taken to Providence Island off the coast of Nicaragua. The prisoners were shackled in a dark, dank, rat-infested prison where most died, including his parents.

David was starving to death and covered with sores when he was rescued by crewmen of Captain Henry Morgan, a bold British privateer. Operating out of Port Royal, Jamaica, in the 1660s, Morgan commanded a large fleet with hundreds of sailors who terrorized the Spanish Main, colonies controlled by Spain in Central and South America and the western Caribbean. England, which was at war with Spain, gave Morgan permission to capture and plunder only Spanish ships. But Morgan found it more profitable to sack towns, even though it was illegal. Spaniards considered him a ruthless pirate; Englishmen hailed him as a heroic privateer.

David admired Morgan. So when he regained his health, the orphaned teenager signed on as a seaman apprentice (a sailor-in-training) aboard Morgan's ship. The freckle-faced redhead had no possessions other than the clothes on his back. What he lacked in worldly goods, he made up for in enthusiasm. Eager to learn, David did more than was asked and worked hard every day. Soon the stocky teenager was promoted to regular seaman status and gained the growing respect of his older shipmates for his intensity and zeal — especially during battle.

Fighting the Spanish was the only way David could channel his seething anger for what they did to him and his family. Although he fell asleep exhausted almost every night, he couldn't prevent the recurring nightmares of that rotten dungeon. It was impossible to rid his mind of the horrid memories of rats gnawing on his chained feet, snakes slithering across his chest, and mold and scum forming on his daily bowl of gruel.

After waking up from another bad dream, David put away his hammock, climbed onto the deck, and gazed at the starry predawn sky. He strolled over to Caleb Jones, a veteran seaman who was on watch, and said, "I'll take over for you."

"Thanks, mate. Mighty nice of you to let me catch some winks. We should be nearing Lake Maracaibo soon."

On this particular voyage, Morgan commanded a fleet of six ships and 400 men with plans to invade towns of Spanish colonists on the large lake in northwest Venezuela. To reach the town of Maracaibo, the fleet would have to fight its way past a heavily armed fort at a narrow inlet that led to Lake Maracaibo. David wasn't afraid. In fact, he relished the upcoming battle because it meant an opportunity for revenge.

The next day, as Morgan's ships neared the fort, the Spaniards unleashed a salvo of cannon fire. As the invaders climbed into rowboats, Caleb told David, "I'll watch your back and you watch mine, right, mate?"

David tapped him with his oar and replied, "Right you are, Caleb."

Geysers from cannonballs showered Morgan's men but didn't slow them down. When the invaders reached the shore, the shelling unexpectedly stopped. Cautiously, they hiked toward the fort through choking smoke from small fires set in their path. Reaching the fort, they discovered it was abandoned.

"The blokes have fled into the woods, the scaredy-cats," Caleb smirked.

"Something's not right," Captain Morgan cautioned. "The fort is too well equipped for them to run. Smells like a trap to me." To his men, he ordered, "Search every room, every corner, every stairway."

Caleb and four others followed David down stone steps into

a cellar and entered a big room where gunpowder was stored in large casks (barrels) and scattered thick throughout the floor. David's nose twitched from a faint burning smell, and his ears detected a slight hiss.

Then he saw it. A smoldering flame was moving rapidly along a fuse and was now only a few inches from reaching the gunpowder. "Aaaahhh!" he shrieked. He leaped on the lit fuse and smothered it before it could ignite a devastating explosion that would have killed him and an untold number of his fellow privateers.

David was still trembling when Morgan slapped the teenager's back and praised him for a job well done. "We would have been blown to pieces, and the fort with us, if it hadn't been for you," said Morgan.

The captain ordered the men to dismantle the 16 cannons, some of which were capable of firing 24-pound iron balls up to 1,000 yards away. The men threw the heavy guns off the fortress walls and burned the wooden gun carriages. They spiked the cannons by driving a nail in the touch hole (the igniter) so the weapons couldn't be fired and buried the guns in the sand.

The following day, the fleet arrived at Maracaibo. To the privateers' surprise, the town was deserted except for a few elderly and disabled people. In halting Spanish, David asked a gnarled old woman, "Where is everyone?"

"In the woods," she replied. "They saw you coming and ran away."

Morgan and his men looted Maracaibo and then invaded the town of Gibraltar on the other side of the lake. Once again, the place was deserted. Wary of another trick from the crafty

Spaniards, Morgan ordered a search of every house and the surrounding area to confirm there were no hidden soldiers ready to ambush them. Assured that the town was empty, the men made themselves comfortable in the vacant houses — after first seizing anything of value.

David took up residence in a comfy thatch-roofed hut. It had rough-hewn furniture and a real bed with a straw mattress. He looked forward to a deep sleep, but tossed and turned through the night. The house triggered too many painful feelings of how much he missed his parents and his once happy childhood back in England.

Because of his sleeping problems, David volunteered as a lookout on the midnight to three A.M. shift atop the church steeple in the center of town. Most every night, he watched his mates sing, dance, and drink. Sometimes they tore down a house or set one on fire just for the fun of it — vandalism they called "the devil's carnival."

During the day for the next three weeks, patrols went out in the woods and captured frightened townspeople who had been holed up in nearby caves. Men, women, and children were imprisoned in the town's main church. Under torture or the threat of it, the captives revealed the locations of their stashed valuables and the hiding places of their relatives and friends.

Once Morgan was satisfied that his men had gathered all the booty they could from Gibraltar, he made plans for his fleet to leave the lake.

That afternoon, David was resting in his hut when a short, middle-aged man appeared in his doorway. Startled, David leaped to his feet, whipped out his dagger, and threw the man to the ground.

"Don't hurt me!" the man cried out.

"Who are you and what are you doing here?"

"This is my house. I came back because I have nowhere else to go. I'm hungry and thirsty. Please help me."

"Why should I?"

"I have important information. Please, a little food and water, and I will tell you all I know."

David marched the man to Captain Morgan, who demanded that the man reveal his information before getting anything to eat or drink.

"I saw three Spanish men-of-war [big naval warships] at the mouth of the lake. They're lying in wait for you, Captain. And many soldiers have returned to the fort with new guns. Is that good information? Is it worth feeding a starving, parched man?"

"Get him some food and water," Morgan directed David. "If we find out he's lying, kill him."

Morgan's spies returned the next evening and confirmed everything. The three warships — the *Magdalena*, the *San Luis* and the *Marquesa* — had a total of 110 large guns and more than 500 troops. The fort also looked well defended with hundreds of soldiers and 16 cannons trained on the narrow channel.

Morgan's largest vessel had only 14 cannons. The rest of the fleet was a motley group of captured merchant ships with few or small guns.

When David heard the news, he felt uneasy. *We're trapped,* he thought. *There's no way we can outgun them. We can't go farther inland and, if we try to flee through the woods, where will we go? Even if we could march to the coast, what would we do next? We won't have any ships.* Gibraltar was uncommonly quiet that night. There was no raucous devil's carnival. Each man was thinking the same thing David was: *How are we going to escape?*

Sensing an atmosphere of gloom, Morgan walked among his men with an air of confidence and fearlessness that buoyed their spirits. "I have thought it over," he told them. "The Spanish believe they have us at their mercy. But I don't. I will prepare a letter to the vice admiral of the warships stating that if they do not allow us free passage out to sea, we will burn every house in Gibraltar."

The men cheered. "We knew we could count on you, Captain," said Caleb.

The Spaniard who had shown up at David's doorstep delivered Morgan's letter to the vice admiral. Two days later, the Spaniard returned with a written response that Morgan read to his men:

"If you will surrender all that you have taken, including prisoners, I will let you pass. If you do not surrender within two days, I will order my troops to destroy you and put every man to the sword. This is my final resolution. Take heed, and be grateful for my kindness. My valiant soldiers yearn to avenge the unrighteous acts you have committed against the Spanish nation.

"Signed on board His Majesty's Ship, *Magdalena*, at anchor in the entrance of Lake Maracaibo, 24 April 1669, Don Alonso del Campo y Espinosa."

After reading the letter to his men, Morgan told them, "There is no exit except through the narrow straits of the lake where the warships lay and where their heavy guns can do us the greatest damage. So, the question is this, gentlemen: Would you rather give up our booty to gain a free passage or try to fight our way out?"

To a man, they chanted, "Fight! Fight! Fight!"

I've risked my life for this booty once and I'm ready to do it again, David thought.

"You have spoken, men, and I most certainly agree," Morgan said. "I will come up with a plan to get us through the blockade."

The next morning, Morgan ordered the men to turn a vessel that they had captured earlier into a fireship — a floating bomb. The plan called for the fireship to lead the convoy and strike the admiral's warship and blow it up in a fiery blast. Morgan's fleet would sail through and then battle the soldiers at the fort.

Working feverishly, the crew made the vessel into a fake pirate ship that looked like one the Spaniards would want to capture. On the deck, the men nailed five-foot-tall logs on end and dressed them in hats and jackets taken from the prisoners of the town. That way the logs would, from a distance, look like sailors. The men cut out portholes on the sides of the vessel and stuck large hollow logs through them, making it look like those logs were cannons.

Next, the men filled the hold with palm leaves and flammable materials that they had collected in town. They spread gunpowder throughout the vessel and sawed up half the woodwork inside the vessel so that it could blow up and burn with greater force.

When the fireship was ready, Morgan asked for 12 volunteers to sail it. The mission was dangerous, requiring split-second timing and lots of luck. One slip-up likely meant death. David didn't hesitate to volunteer. Neither did Caleb.

Before the fleet set sail, David and every other seaman took an oath: "We will stand by our brothers to the last drop of blood. Whatever fate may decree, we will never cry for quarter [mercy] but fight to the last man."

At dawn, Morgan's six vessels — including one full of prisoners — set sail, trailing behind the fireship. David felt jumpy yet excited. *Everything has to go perfectly,* he thought, *or I will be nothing but ash.*

The three Spanish vessels were soon in sight. "Steady as she goes," Caleb told the pilot of the fireship. "Good, they're not firing on us. They want us to get closer so they can board us. They've fallen for our ruse. Start making noise, mates."

David and the 11 others began shouting and scurrying around the deck to give the impression that there were many pirates on board. The running and yelling helped David vent the nervous energy that had built up inside him. As the fireship pulled alongside the *Magdalena*, the privateers flung their grapples (light anchors with sharp barbs). The ropes of the grapples were attached to the fireship, so when the barbs dug deep into the wood decking of the Spanish vessel, the ships became hooked together.

Then the daring dozen ran about the fireship, lighting fuses here and there. As the Spanish sailors charged onto the vessel, David and his mates leaped over the other side. He was still in the air when the first explosion rocked the fire ship, buffeting him with enough force to flip him. He hit the water hard on his back, momentarily stunning him. A series of thunderous blasts then ripped apart both ships. Debris rained down, forcing David to swim underwater to avoid getting hit.

All 12 men reached the second ship in Morgan's fleet. When they were hauled aboard, their fellow seamen cheered them.

"We did it, Caleb!" David shouted. "Huzzah! We blew her up exactly the way we planned. Huzzah!" He watched with satisfying fascination as the flaming *Magdalena* listed to her side and sank.

Meanwhile, the other two Spanish vessels had troubles of their own. The *San Luis* sped off toward the fort for protection, but in her haste ran aground. The Spaniards frantically took what valuables they could out of her before setting her on fire so Morgan's men couldn't steal her. The *Marquesa* tried to run off, but two of Morgan's fastest ships chased her and captured her after a bloody fight.

David was in awe. Although Morgan's men had been outgunned and outmanned and seemingly trapped in the lake, it took only two hours for them to destroy the Spanish blockade. But there was no time to savor this amazing victory. Another big battle still loomed — the assault on the fort.

Still in his wet clothes, David joined his mates as they rowed to shore under heavy artillery fire. They had only their muskets and a few hand grenades, because their ships' cannons were too small to damage the fort's strong walls. The fighting lasted most of the day until Morgan's men retreated when the

Spaniards began hurling fireballs — red-hot cannonballs — and pots of gunpowder tied to lighted fuses.

The invaders, who suffered dozens of injuries and 30 deaths, regrouped on their ships and went to Maracaibo. David's legs were battered and bleeding, and Caleb's face and arms were red from burns.

After learning from a prisoner that the *Magdalena* was carrying a large amount of silver, Morgan asked for volunteers to salvage her. David was soon back in the water, swimming into the gaping holes of the submerged man-of-war's hull. He and the other divers brought up 15,000 pieces of eight (old Spanish coins worth eight reals) and silver daggers and plates. Some of the coins had melted together in the intense heat from the fire, forming heavy clumps that weighed as much as 30 pounds.

The coins, jewels, and silver were probably worth about 250,000 pieces of eight. Morgan personally gave David and the other 11 men on the fireship mission part of an extra share for their bravery.

"You have shown courage far beyond your years, lad," Morgan told him.

"Thank you, Captain," said David. "This has been the greatest day of my life."

"May your life be long and prosperous."

There was still the matter of how the fleet would get past the fort without being bombarded into oblivion. As always, Morgan had a plan. He told his prisoners they had to convince Vice Admiral del Campo, who had fled to the fort after the *Magdalena* caught fire, to let the fleet pass the fort safely or else they would be hanged. The prisoners sent a messenger to Don Alonso, pleading with him to let Morgan's men go free because the lives of many women and children were at stake.

When the messenger returned with the admiral's response, Morgan informed his men, "Del Campo is a fool. Rather than be concerned for the lives of his countrymen, he called them cowards. He says that had the people fought us, we never could have sacked Maracaibo or Gibraltar. He claims that on no account will he allow us safe passage. On the contrary, he promises to send every last one of us to the bottom." The men booed and hissed.

"The question of getting away is a serious one. Our fleet consists of small vessels that cannot defy the guns of the fort. As stout of heart and brawny of arm that you are, we will need our brains to solve this dilemma."

Morgan will come up with a plan, David thought. *He always does.*

The next day, the fleet left Maracaibo with their booty and prisoners. Soon they anchored in the lake far enough from the fort to be safe from its guns, but close enough for the Spaniards to watch the seamen's movements. Each ship dispatched rowboats filled with armed men to a wooded shore on the same side as the fort a half mile away. Instead of getting out, though, the men crouched in the bottom of the boats so that they couldn't be seen. The boats, which to the Spaniards seemed empty except for a few rowers, returned to the ships. This performance was repeated several times.

Later, Morgan's spies returned with good news. Just as the captain had hoped, the hoax had convinced the Spaniards that his privateers would attack the fort from the rear by land later that night. Del Campo ordered all his big cannons moved from the lakeside to the landside of the fort, and posted most of his soldiers so they faced the rear, waiting for the invaders to make their expected assault.

When it turned dark and with the tide running out, Morgan's fleet weighed anchor (raised their anchors) and drifted silently toward the fort. David, who was in the second ship of the convoy, kept his eyes glued to the fort. *If Morgan's trick gets discovered, we'll be blown to smithereens*, he thought.

Fortunately, the Spaniards didn't notice the fleet, because they were at the back of the fort, bracing for an attack that never happened. As the ships slowly sneaked past the walls of the fort, Morgan gave the signal for every vessel to cut her sails (let them unfurl). Propelled by a favorable wind, they glided toward the open sea. The last vessel had scarcely passed the fort when the Spaniards discovered the scheme. They rolled their cannons back to face the water and began firing, but it was too late.

When they were out of range, Morgan's ships dropped anchor and let the prisoners take one of the boats back to Maracaibo. As a parting insult, Morgan, who had made the captured *Marquesa* his flagship, fired eight cannons. The humiliated enemy chose not to respond.

On deck, the men gave raucous cheers. "We did it!" shouted David. "We bamboozled the Spaniards! Now let's go home. I've got booty to spend."

*   *   *

The fleet reached Port Royal, Jamaica, in May, where most of the men wasted their money in taverns and gambling joints.

Morgan became the most successful raider of his era by continuing to sack towns in the Spanish Main. He became extremely wealthy and influential in island politics, owning several plantations in Jamaica. In 1674, the king appointed Morgan lieutenant governor of the island.

David (whose real name has been lost to history) remained a member of Morgan's crew for several years before settling down to a normal life in Jamaica.

This story is based on an eyewitness account of the Maracaibo raid and escape by Morgan's Dutch-born crewman, Alexander Exquemelin, who wrote The Buccaneers of America *in 1678.*

TURNING BACK THE TURNCOATS

RICHARD BARLEYCORN,
CABIN BOY FOR CAPTAIN WILLIAM KIDD

Cursing and yelling, the pirates banged on the captain's door. "Give us the gold, you scalawag! Give us our share, or we'll kill you!"

They pounded harder. But the door, which was barricaded with heavy bales of fabric, held firm. Inside, Captain William Kidd and his loyal cabin boy, Richard Barleycorn, were feverishly loading pistols and single-shot rifles called muskets. "If they bust down the door," Kidd whispered to Richard, "just keep feeding me a charged [loaded] weapon as fast as you can."

Richard nodded. He couldn't talk. Fear had locked his jaws.

"If you want it, come and get it!" Kidd challenged the pirates. "But I'll blow away the first man who breaks in here!"

"You can't kill all of us," a voice retorted. "We'll get through, and you'll pay with your life!"

This is not the way I expected to die, Richard thought. *Killed by my fellow mates.*

* * *

"Come on, Richard, it'll be fun," declared his pal Saunders Douglas. "We've been working in this dingy tavern for more than a year. At least as cabin boys for Captain Kidd, we can get out of here and see the world."

It was the summer of 1696 in New York. Richard and Saunders, both 13, had just been told by their employer that he had arranged for them to serve on a voyage to hunt pirates in the Indian Ocean. Richard was uneasy about sailing, but he agreed.

The boys joined three other teenage apprentices (trainees) aboard the *Adventure Galley*, a three-masted, 32-gun warship manned by a crew of 152 mostly English, Dutch, and Scottish sailors and former pirates. Their commander, William Kidd, was a rowdy forceful Scotsman who dressed well and wore a shoulder-length wig. King William of England had given him a letter of marque, an official document directing him to hunt pirates and vessels of France, which was England's enemy. Kidd had the right to steal from pirates and the French without returning the stolen goods to their rightful owner. Whatever booty he collected had to be shared among his crew, his financial backers, and the king. But he was not permitted to attack British ships or vessels belonging to friends of England.

On September 6, 1696, Richard watched New York disappear on the horizon as the *Adventure Galley* headed out to sea. His stomach swirled with butterflies over the uncertainty of his new life. Saunders playfully punched Richard in the arm and said, "Smile, my friend. We're off for a grand time!"

Within a couple of days, everyone was required to sign Kidd's 18 articles of agreement — the rules of the ship. For those like Richard who couldn't read or write, the articles were read aloud to them, and they signed by making an "X." Among the articles:

- If any man loses an eye, leg, or arm, he shall receive 600 pieces of eight or six able slaves.
- If anyone disobeys his superior officer, he shall lose his share or receive such physical punishment as the captain and majority of the crew shall deem fit.
- If anyone is proved a coward in time of battle, he shall lose his share.
- If any man shall hide from the crew any treasure, he shall lose his share and be put on shore upon the first inhabited island.
- All money and treasure taken by the crew shall be shared immediately and legally divided among the crew.

Richard became the personal aide to the captain — working as a servant, errand boy, and messenger. He was quick to anticipate what Kidd needed and usually had to be told only once to carry out an order. Although the blond, blue-eyed cabin boy was short and stocky, he moved with surprising swiftness and agility. The captain liked Richard and spent time teaching him to read and write.

Saunders, meanwhile, was an aide to the quartermaster (the second-in-command) and was a budding seaman. The lanky, always-smiling teen was a fast learner and planned to spend the rest of his life sailing the oceans.

When the ship crossed the equator, the veteran seamen

held a ritual for all first-time sailors like Richard. "It's time for you boys to get baptized," the quartermaster said after the crew had gathered on deck. The seamen slipped a rope through a pulley of a yardarm, the far end of a horizontal pole that suspends a sail. "Who is man enough among you sea babies to be the first?" the quartermaster asked.

"I'm not sure what they're going to do, but I don't like the looks of this," Richard murmured to Saunders.

His pal shrugged and whispered back, "Me, neither, but they're going to baptize us whether we like it or not." Saunders stepped forward and shouted, "I'll go first!"

The men tied him in a harness and hoisted him 40 feet in the air until he was dangling beneath the yardarm out over the blue Atlantic. Then they released the rope and watched Saunders plunge into the water. Twice more they lifted him up and dropped him again into the sea. After he was hauled onto the deck, the dripping wet boy yelled, "Huzzah! That was fun!" The men cheered and fired off their guns in a show of respect.

When it was Richard's turn, he yelled all the way up to the yardarm and all the way down into the water. Because he couldn't stop screaming, he was dunked four times. "I hope there aren't any other rituals," he told Saunders later.

Five months into the voyage, after they had entered the Indian Ocean, Richard felt the tension building among the increasingly frustrated crew. For good reason. They had yet to find a pirate or a French ship. And the *Adventure Galley* was leaking badly, forcing the sailors to pump out water around the clock. It was Richard's job to flip the hourglass over and alert the next shift to go below and pump.

Kidd deliberately beached the ship on an island off Madagascar so the men could repair the vessel. Saunders, who loved to climb, was part of a team that attached ropes and pulleys to trees on the shore so they could yank the vessel onto her side and work on her hull. Swinging from one tree to another on a rope, Saunders yelled, "Look, I'm skylarking!" The others laughed, but Kidd wasn't amused and ordered him to do his job.

After they removed many of the cannons — some weighing as much as a ton each — and tied down cargo and provisions, they flopped the boat on her side. Then the crewmen scraped off barnacles, shells that stick to the hull and slow a ship down. The sailors also patched holes bored by tropical sea worms. The seams between the hull's planks, which gradually spread open from the pounding of waves, were packed with oakum, fibers from old rope soaked in tar. When that task was done, the crew flipped the boat over on her other side and repeated the lengthy, backbreaking work.

Halfway through the maintenance, Saunders contracted a tropical disease. There was no potion, no drug, no treatment that could cure him from the flux, as the seamen called it. Back then, ships had "surgeons" who weren't doctors but rather sailors or barbers who had some medical knowledge. In desperation, the *Adventure Galley*'s surgeon cut open one of Saunders's veins, hoping to bleed "the bad stuff" out of him. Slumped against the base of a palm tree, Saunders told Richard, "Every day I'm feeling worse. I can't hold anything in my stomach. I'm getting weak. Look at me, Richard. I'm shivering, and it's a hundred degrees in the shade."

Richard tried to feed him a mashed banana, but Saunders couldn't swallow. "I'll find something else for you," Richard said. He returned with a cut lime that he planned to squeeze into his friend's parched mouth. But Saunders was slumped over. Richard dropped to his knees and wept. His best friend was dead.

The disease quickly spread, and soon more than 100 men fell sick. They were moaning and sprawled out under trees, their arms bandaged from the surgeon's bloodletting. But the treatment didn't work. Within a week, 40 men had died.

Richard, his mind numb from grief, helped dig the grave of his pal and watched tearfully as they laid him to rest. Then the men went back to work on the boat, stopping only to bury more of their mates.

After the ship was repaired and the supplies restocked, the surviving crewmen, who all had regained their health, went hunting for a prize (a ship to capture). It had been nine months without a capture or pay, and Richard began hearing whispers that it was time to raid a ship, any ship.

The *Adventure Galley* soon stopped the *Mary*, a merchant ship that proved to be an English vessel captained by Thomas Parker and crewed by 12 Moors, native people from India. For more than an hour in his cabin, Kidd entertained Parker, neither one knowing that some of Kidd's crew who were former pirates had boarded the *Mary*. They ransacked the ship and took bales of coffee, navigation instruments, clothes, rice, and six muskets.

Richard had been serving drinks and food to the two captains when he heard screams coming from the *Mary*. He went up on deck and saw 10 of his mates torturing two Moors into revealing where more booty was hidden. The victims' arms were tied behind their backs, and their bodies had been hoisted a few inches off the deck. Kidd's crewmen were slapping them hard with the flat side of their knives. Richard knew that if either Moor flinched from a slap, the blade would cut him.

Richard rushed into Kidd's quarters and told him what was happening. Kidd was furious and ordered his men to return all that they had stolen. "We are *not* pirates!" he bellowed. Only because of the sheer force of his leadership did they obey — although grudgingly.

Months later, the *Adventure Galley* stopped another ship, the *Loyal Captain*, which also turned out to be English, much to the frustration of Kidd's crew. In his cabin, Kidd was hosting the commander of the other ship while the seamen from both vessels talked to one another. Kidd's crew learned that the *Loyal Captain*'s passengers were Greek merchants carrying silver and diamonds.

From behind a water cask, Richard listened to William Moore, the *Adventure Galley*'s gunner and a former pirate, plotting with a few dozen mates. "We've been living for a year at sea with nothing to show for it," he complained. "We're hungry for some riches." Pointing to the *Loyal Captain*, he said, "Men, it's right over there. Like apples on a tree, it's ready for the picking." His mates agreed and planned to sneak over.

Without thinking, Richard stepped forward and shouted, "You can't do that!"

"Oh, it's our captain's cabin boy trying to act like a brave mariner," snarled Moore. "Are you going to stop us?" Moore strode over to Richard and slapped him across the face with the back of his hand, sending the boy reeling against the barrel.

Dazed and bleeding, Richard staggered to his feet. *What do I do now?* he wondered. *I can't stop them. They'll kill me if I try.*

Hearing the commotion, Kidd bounded onto the deck and confronted the crew. When he learned of their scheme, he declared, "You will do no such thing! Our letter of marque says we take only pirates and French ships."

"You treat us like galley slaves, and for what?" growled Moore. "We're taking matters into our own hands. We've voted. A majority says plunder the English ship." Raising their knives and pistols, the others backed him with their shouts. Moore motioned for the men to board the *Loyal Captain*.

"You dare not do such a thing," Kidd insisted.

"We should do it," Moore claimed. "We're beggars already."

"Oh? You think it's right to take this ship because we are poor?"

"You have brought us to ruin!"

"If you are so bent on taking her, then go ahead. But if you board her, you are on your own and can never come aboard this ship again."

Grumbling, Moore and the others backed down. The pain that Richard felt when Moore struck him was dulled by his awe for the captain. *Most of the crew is against him, but he's still in control. Amazing.*

After 14 months at sea, the *Adventure Galley* finally captured a merchant ship flying a French flag. But when Kidd examined her papers, he discovered she was an Indian-owned vessel carrying Dutch cargo. Over his objections, the men voted overwhelmingly to keep the ship as a legal prize and seize her cargo of two dozen bales of cotton, 50 quilts, and the household furnishings of a Dutch official. It wasn't much, but it was something.

Several Dutch sailors willingly joined Kidd's crew. But natives who had been working on the Dutch ship were forced to man the pumps of the *Adventure Galley*, which was leaking again. The rest of the Dutchmen were allowed to row six miles to shore. The captured ship was renamed the *November* in honor of the month of the crew's first prize. The two boats sailed to a smuggler's port and, with money from the sale of the booty, bought needed food and other supplies.

Richard heard no more talk of mutiny, although the crew kept griping after each day passed without a new capture. But on January 30, 1698, they finally snared a rich prize — the merchant ship *Quedagh Merchant*. She was a vessel from Armenia, but because her owner carried several passes, including one from France, Kidd decided the seizure was legal. The ship contained 600 bales of expensive fabric and other goods.

During a search of the ship, Richard found a wooden chest strapped with iron and double padlocked. Before opening it, Kidd cleared the room of everyone but Richard. Using a chisel and hammer, they broke the locks. When they opened it, they found little leather pouches containing rubies, emeralds, diamonds, gold nuggets, silver rings, and gold jewelry. Kidd scattered the dazzling jewels on the table and sifted through them.

"They're beautiful," said Richard in wonder. "I've never seen anything so sparkly in my life. They look like they could belong to a princess."

Kidd put the precious stones back in their bags and locked them in the chest. He looked Richard in the eye and said, "Not a word of the contents to anyone."

Richard nodded, and together they hid the chest in the captain's cabin.

Kidd now had three vessels in his fleet, but his flagship, the *Adventure Galley*, was in danger of sinking because the seams on the hull were opening up. The men wrapped the ship in very thick ropes, which held her together until they reached the smuggler's port of St. Mary's, another island off the coast of Madagascar.

Like so many times before, Richard started hearing complaints because his mates hadn't received their share of the booty from the *Quedagh Merchant*. Fueling their growing restlessness was news that successful English pirate Robert Culliford was somewhere on the island. His ship, the *Resolution*, was anchored nearby while he and his crew were partying for weeks at a village several miles inland.

Meanwhile, the *Adventure Galley* underwent repairs. Richard could feel the tension growing among the men, who despised their captain for making them work so hard without sharing the booty. So when Kidd gathered them aboard his flagship to tell them of a new plan, Richard wondered how they would react.

Armed with two pistols and his sword, Kidd stood on the poop deck (the raised rear deck) and told the crew, "We have enough manpower and cannon power to blast Culliford into submission. And we have the authority. We will take his ship and his men and return them to England. So what do you say, men?"

But instead of cheers there was silence, finally broken by a seaman who shouted, "We would rather fire two guns into you than one into Culliford." A gruff approval erupted from the main deck. Then another crewman yelled, "Where's our money? It's been almost two years at sea, and we want some real pay."

"Now is the time to fight Culliford," Kidd claimed. "We'll all be richer."

"We want our shares now!" the seamen roared.

"You'll get them when we get back to New York. Not before."

This is turning ugly, Richard thought. *The men are really angry.* He was right. A short while later, the crew voted 100 to 15 to leave Kidd and join forces with Culliford — but only after they divided the spoils from the *Quedagh Merchant.*

Each man received three bales of fabric, marking them with their initials or, for the illiterate ones, their own mark. Richard proudly wrote a large RB — because he had learned how to read and write, thanks to his captain. He hoped to sell his bales when they returned to England, whenever that might be. But he had a more pressing concern — staying alive.

The number of seamen who remained loyal to Kidd was a ragtag group of cabin boys, old men, sick men, and a few able-bodied sailors. They were powerless to stop the deserters from looting Kidd's three ships. For five days, the turncoats carried away cannons, gunpowder, ammunition, small arms, sails, anchors, the ship's medicine chest, and whatever else they pleased.

Will they come after us next for sticking with the captain? Richard wondered.

After the deserters had taken everything they wanted, they turned their attention to stealing the captain's treasure chest.

Harry Lane, one of the deserters who went his own way but was friendly to Richard, told the cabin boy, "Do you know where Kidd's treasure chest is? Tell me, and we'll split it. Just the two of us."

Richard shook his head. "Sorry, but I'm just his cabin boy. I don't know where the chest is — or even if there is one," he lied.

Harry snarled at him. "Well, then, it's your funeral. They plan to sneak into the captain's cabin and slit his throat. And yours, too, if you get in their way."

Richard pretended he wasn't fazed, although his knees nearly buckled from the terror he now felt. He rushed to the captain's quarters and told him of the threat. He and Kidd hurriedly barricaded the door with bales of fabric and frantically loaded 40 small arms and two dozen pistols.

"You don't have to shoot anyone," Kidd told Richard. "Leave that to me. Just keep handing me a charged weapon."

Within minutes, the deserters were banging on the captain's door, yelling, "Give us the gold! We know you're hiding it in there!"

"Come in and get it if you've got the guts, because I'm armed to the teeth!" Kidd retorted.

For three frightening days and nights — the longest in the young cabin boy's life — the deserters took turns pounding on the door and trying to pry it open. But no one had the nerve to storm inside.

"If you bust in here," the captain warned them, "I'll blow up the ship and send us all sky-high. And you know I'm stubborn enough to do it, too."

Richard gulped. *I hope he's bluffing.*

On the fourth day of the siege, the deserters unexpectedly left for good to join Culliford who was weighing anchor to begin a new search for prey from any nation. As a parting shot to Kidd, someone poured alcohol on the deck of the *Adventure Galley* and set it on fire. While Richard and Kidd remained in their barricaded quarters, two loyal mates snuffed out the fire. But there was nothing they could do when Culliford's men burned the *November* on their way out of the harbor.

When Richard emerged from the cabin, he could hardly walk. He was mentally and physically drained. Kidd, on the other hand, seemed buoyant because he had saved his treasure.

Kidd decided that the only way home was to sail the *Quedagh Merchant.* The deserters had pillaged her of sails, anchors, and rigging. But they had left about 300 bales of expensive fabric. Using material from the bales and scraps from the remaining sails, the older sailors sewed enough together to make two sets of sails.

Kidd's small crew scavenged the *Adventure Galley*, dismantling her masts, spars, and rigging. They transferred the provisions and water casks as well as 30 cannons. They wouldn't have the manpower to fire all the guns, but by adding the cannons, the vessel looked like an intimidating warship.

After three hard months, the ship was ready to sail. To his crew of 22 veteran sailors (including a few who joined him from other ships that had visited the island), five boys, and a handful of young slaves, Kidd said, "We survived disease, desertion, and rotten luck. We've gone through bad times and even worse times. It's time to go home."

Amen to that, thought Richard. *Amen.*

The crew eventually made it to Boston near where Captain Kidd reportedly buried his treasure. But it wasn't a happy homecoming. Kidd, Richard, and five others were arrested on piracy charges involving the Quedagh Merchant *and sent to London to stand trial. They pleaded their innocence. The jury found Richard and two other cabin boys not guilty. However, the other four were convicted and sentenced to death. They were hanged on May 23, 1701, at London's Execution Dock. Kidd's body was then suspended in an iron cage on the banks of the Thames River as a warning to other pirates.*

What ever happened to Richard Barleycorn? No one knows for sure.

SADDER BUT WISER

LOUIS AROT,
CABIN BOY FOR PIRATE BLACKBEARD

Louis Arot didn't know how much longer he could stand it. Day after day, he helped carry the sick and the dying up on the deck of the slave ship *Concorde* for a little fresh air. That was the best he could do for the victims of scurvy — the scourge of seamen for centuries.

The fatal disease, caused by a lack of vitamin C, was spreading throughout the ship because there were no fresh fruits and vegetables. And there was no way to get any, because the vessel was stuck in calm seas in the middle of nowhere in the Atlantic, her sails limp from days without even a puff of breeze.

Louis could hardly stand to look at the listless, pain-racked victims whose arms and legs were swollen, their skin covered in dark splotches, their eyes glazed. He would turn his head when they parted their withered lips and showed black, swollen gums and loose teeth. He knew that within a day or two they would be gasping for breath like floundered fish and die.

31

I feel so helpless, the 14-year-old thought. *I wish I had never got on this slaver.*

Louis had signed on as a cabin boy on the *Concorde*, a 100-foot-long slave ship armed with 16 cannons and a crew of 75. The ship left his hometown of Nantes, France, on March 24, 1717. On July 8, it arrived at the West African port of Ouidah — the center for slave trading at the time — and took on a cargo of 516 captive Africans. The ship was scheduled to transport them across the Atlantic to the West Indies in the Caribbean, where they would be sold as slaves for the sugarcane plantations.

As Louis helped load the ship, he heard Captain Pierre Dosset and one of the ship's officers argue over the amount of fruit and vegetables to carry for the crew and slaves. "Do as I say and cut the order in half!" the captain snapped.

On the day they set sail, Louis noticed that the captain and his four officers were carrying leather bags aboard. He didn't know what was inside them until two weeks into the trip. While cleaning Dosset's cabin, Louis accidentally banged into a wooden post of the captain's bed. The top of the post fell off, revealing a secret hiding place. Inside was a leather bag. Curious, Louis untied the bag. *It's gold dust!* Coming from a poor family, Louis had never held such wealth in his hands. *There's more than a whole year's worth of a seaman's wages. Oh, what I could do with this gold.* Before he could daydream any longer, he heard footsteps. He quickly tied up the bag, slipped it into the hollowed-out bedpost, and put the top back on moments before the captain entered the room.

Louis, a strapping teenager with shaggy black hair that

covered his ears and eyebrows, spent his free time learning all he could from the crew about sailing a ship. He tried to stay busy because he didn't want to think about the cargo of human misery in the hold beneath his feet. *I'll be so glad to reach the West Indies*, he thought.

Then the winds died. Trapped in an area of the Atlantic where there were no currents, the *Concorde* didn't move. Louis tossed a piece of wood and a chunk of rope over the side and watched them float to measure the ship's slow progress. To his dismay, these same objects still were nearby a week later. For five weeks, six weeks, seven weeks, every day was the same — sunny, hot, and dry. And maddeningly calm.

Food and water were running out. But Louis knew that the captain and the four officers were never as hungry or thirsty as the rest. As a cabin boy, he fetched the five of them food and wine from a secret stash of supplies. He didn't steal any for himself, but he did eat what few crumbs and tiny leftovers were on their plates.

Soon after the supply of fruit or vegetables had been exhausted, the first signs of scurvy appeared in crewmembers and slaves. The infected ones began shivering, then cursing and weeping the sicker they became. Their cries turned to moans, and then they died.

Louis and the surviving crewmen were racked by hunger and thirst and longed for home. Or at least a breeze. *I hate this life*, he told himself. *I hate this ship. I hate the officers. I hate that people are dying.*

Finally, after another restless night in early November, he awoke to a wondrous sight. The sails were full, the clouds were billowing, and the wind was stiff. The ship was on her way. By now 61 slaves and 16 crewmen had perished. Another 36 crewmen were seriously ill. The only question was how many more would die before they could reach their destination — the island of Martinique.

The *Concorde* was about 100 miles away when a lookout hollered that he had spotted two ships. Like all the crewmen, Louis's hopes soared that the vessels would have extra water and food, maybe even fruit that could save lives.

But his heart sank when the ships drew near. They were flying black flags, each of a skeleton holding a dagger in one hand and an hourglass in the other next to a bleeding heart. *Pirates!* he thought. *We're doomed!*

One of the ships carried 120 men and 12 cannons; the other had 30 men and 8 cannons. The pirates fired two blasts over the bow of the *Concorde* in a signal for her to stop. With the French crew shorthanded by death and illness, they were powerless to resist, so Captain Dosset surrendered without a fight.

When the leader of the pirates stepped aboard, Louis gasped. He was a large man with a long black beard that covered most of his face and flowed to his chest. It was tied with several colorful ribbons. He wore a crimson coat over a crisscrossing harness that held four pistols and two daggers. A sword dangled on each side of his hip. His crew called him Captain Teach. The world knew him as Blackbeard the pirate. He barked orders that his menacing crew carried out with quiet efficiency.

The pirates took the *Concorde* to the island of Bequia in the Grenadines where the French crew and the enslaved Africans were put ashore. While the pirates rummaged through the

Concorde, Blackbeard pulled out a cutlass and walked among the Frenchmen on the beach. "You wouldn't be hiding anything of value, would you?" he asked the captain.

"I have nothing," said Dosset.

"A slaver like you with no valuables? Hard to believe. Are you sure you haven't squirreled some away?"

Blackbeard waved his cutlass, and then his eyes fell on Louis. "Well, laddie, judging from your youth, I imagine you're the cabin boy."

"Yes, sir," gulped Louis.

"As a cabin boy, you must know where the captain keeps everything, right?"

"Yes, sir."

"Then tell me" — he placed his razor-sharp cutlass gently on Louis's neck — "is the captain hiding anything?"

Why should I protect Dosset? thought Louis. *He's a slaver. He could care less about his crew. I don't owe him anything.*

"You want to tell me something, don't you, laddie?" Blackbeard put down the cutlass and ordered a pirate to bring Louis a jug of water. "Here, laddie, drink up."

"Thank you, sir."

After guzzling the entire contents, Louis blurted out, "The captain has gold dust hidden in the post of his bed. The other officers hid pouches of gold dust, too."

"What a fine lad you are," Blackbeard beamed.

Within minutes, the pirates had uncovered the bags of gold. Blackbeard then decided to give the French crew and their slaves the smaller of his two ships while he and his crew took the *Concorde* as their own.

"Who wants to join me?" Blackbeard asked the Frenchmen.

I can't go with Dosset, Louis thought. *He'll flog [whip] me, and the officers will make my life miserable.* Louis stepped forward. "I do, Captain Teach."

Three others joined him. Then Blackbeard took three surgeons, two carpenters, two sailors, and the cook against their will. With the pirates' former ship, the French continued their trip with the surviving slaves to Martinique. Blackbeard added 24 cannons to his captured vessel, now renamed *Queen Anne's Revenge* (the *QAR*, for short), before leaving Bequia in late November. He cruised the Caribbean, capturing prizes and adding to his fleet and his forces, which at one point numbered 400 pirates.

Louis was fascinated by the way Blackbeard would strike terror into the hearts of his victims when he boarded their vessel. Besides his bushy beard, booming voice, and the weapons he carried, he displayed another intimidating touch. He weaved wicks laced with gunpowder into his hair and beard, and lit them so smoke curled out from around his large head.

The sight of a fiery Blackbeard was enough to make most of his victims surrender without a fight. If they gave up peacefully, his crew stole their valuables, navigational instruments, weapons, and rum before letting them go. If they tried to fight, he usually marooned (abandoned) them on an island and burned their ship.

Louis found the life of a pirate exciting at times. When the *QAR* attacked another ship, he carried out the duties of a powder monkey, a boy who runs back and forth across the deck with gunpowder and water for the gunners. But the battles were usually short and the surrenders swift.

Promoted to Blackbeard's assistant, Louis realized that the more he got to know him, the more he thought the pirate was a madman.

Louis's first hint came the day the ship was anchored off Cuba, and Blackbeard announced to his crew, "I have invented a game that we're all going to play. I call it Living in the Lower Regions of the Devil. I want everyone down into the hold."

After they assembled below deck, Blackbeard ordered all the hatches and other openings closed but unlocked. "Let's make our own torment — one that the devil would enjoy — and see how long we can bear it," the pirate said. "Leave when you want, so the rest of us can see how weak you are." Then he filled several pots with brimstone (smelly sulfur in a powdery form) and lighted them.

I don't like this game, Louis thought. As the sulfur burned, the poisonous fumes rose, spreading a ghastly glow throughout the hold. Louis pulled his shirt over his mouth and nose as did other pirates, who began coughing and gagging. Blackbeard laughed at his gasping crew and ignited more brimstone. "I'm just as willing to breathe the devil's fumes as I am the salty sea air," roared Blackbeard.

His eyes stinging and lungs aching, Louis began to panic. *I need to get out of here or else I'm going to die. Why isn't anyone else moving? Are they all as crazy as Blackbeard? Let them laugh at me. I'm leaving.*

He staggered to his feet and climbed out of the hold, flopped onto the deck, and gulped fresh air. Within seconds, all the other pirates scrambled out, retching and hacking until only one was left below — Blackbeard. When he eventually emerged, he addressed his crew with a boast: "I didn't even sneeze. You, though, are nothing but a bunch of yellow-bellied sapsuckers! I'm a tougher man than all you milksops [cowards] put together!"

Blackbeard — who now demanded that everyone call him Commodore — and his men continued to plunder ships throughout the Caribbean, amassing a magnificent booty of gold, silver, and jewels. He also added captured ships to his fleet.

In May 1718, the pirates anchored a few miles off the harbor of Charleston, South Carolina (then called Charles Town), ,and blockaded the port for nearly a week. During the siege, they seized several ships attempting to enter or leave the port. Their biggest prize was the England-bound merchant ship *Crowley*, which carried dozens of men, women, and children from well-off families. Unlike the other vessels, Blackbeard kept the crew and passengers of the *Crowley* as prisoners.

"There are eight sail [ships] in the harbor, ready for the sea, but none dare venture out because it is impossible to escape my clutches," Blackbeard boasted to his crew. Pointing toward the open ocean, he added, "Those vessels that want to come into port are under the same unhappy dilemma. They will have to deal with me if they want to continue trading with Charleston. I will go down in infamy as the greatest pirate of them all!" His men cheered. So did Louis.

The prisoners were taken aboard the *QAR*, where the men were questioned about their possessions. "It will be death for any man who tells a lie or otherwise evades the question," Blackbeard threatened.

Once the *Crowley* had been stripped of everything of value, the prisoners were put back aboard their own ship, where they still were held captive. Louis helped usher several crying children onto the *Crowley*. When a five-year-old boy became separated from his parents and began wailing, Louis pulled him aside and sang a little song to calm him. Then Louis searched among the prisoners until he found the boy's parents.

The teary-eyed mother hugged her sniffling son. Then she grabbed Louis by the arm and in a trembling voice said, "You're going to kill all of us, aren't you?"

"No, madam, we don't kill innocent people," he replied.

The boy's father whispered to Louis, "Tell Blackbeard I am Samuel Wragg, a member of the colonial council in Charleston. I am an important person and I can arrange a ransom to be paid in exchange for sparing our lives."

Before he could say anything else, other pirates shoved the prisoners down into the *Crowley*'s hold, locked all the hatches, and jumped back on the *QAR*. Louis could hear the prisoners, who were convinced they were about to die, plead, "Don't blow us up! Don't sink us! Have mercy!"

Louis rushed to Blackbeard's quarters and told him about Wragg's offer to help. The pirate was intrigued. "We don't really need any more gold or silver, now do we?" he said. "We are flush with riches."

"If you please, Commodore, I wish to make a suggestion."

Blackbeard squinted his eyes, wondering whether he should bother to listen to such a lowly crewmember. Somewhat annoyed, he said, "What is it?"

"Well, Commodore, our surgeons are complaining about the lack of medicine." Referring to an intestinal ailment that was spreading among the fleet, Louis continued, "Every day more seamen go down from dysentery. . . ."

"Aha!" Blackbeard said. "I have an excellent idea. Tell the chief surgeon to draw up a list of all the potions, pills, and medications he desires. We will demand as ransom from Charleston that they fill our medicine chest until it is the finest in all the Atlantic."

Slapping Louis hard on the back, he said, "Bring me Mr. Wragg and a man he thinks can be trusted with their lives."

After Louis escorted Wragg and Charleston businessman Arnold Marks to the pirate's cabin, Blackbeard said, "Mr. Marks, we are in need of medicines from the governor in Charleston. Our chief surgeon has prepared a list. You and three of my loyal men will visit the governor and obtain from him all the requested medicine, which you will deliver to me within forty-eight hours."

"And why would the good governor provide medicine to pirates like you?" Marks asked defiantly.

Blackbeard smiled, but with each word the smile grew into a scowl. "If you do not return with all the medicines, I will see to it personally that every prisoner — every man, woman, and child — is hanged from the yardarm of the *Crowley*. And then I will scuttle [sink] every ship in the harbor."

He wouldn't really, would he? Louis thought. *I've never seen him kill anybody except in battle. Could he murder innocent, helpless women and children? I don't know. Maybe he's crazy enough to do it.*

"But I should be the one going ashore to get the medicine," said Wragg.

"No," Blackbeard said. "You will remain my 'guest' because I will hold you responsible if anything goes wrong. Pray it doesn't. If your man Marks fails, I will have your head delivered to the governor." The pirate turned over an hourglass that was sitting on his desk. "You better get going, Mr. Marks. Time is wasting."

Two days later when the deadline had passed, there was no sign of Marks or the three pirates. From his cabin, Blackbeard ordered Louis to bring him Wragg.

When they arrived, the pirate pulled out a dagger, drove it deep into his table, and snarled, "Mr. Wragg, I will not be trifled with. I sense that some foul treachery was played on my men, that the governor has refused to pay the ransom and has imprisoned them. The deadline has come and gone. I am nothing if not a man of my word. Therefore, I will carry out the consequence of this defiance — immediate death to all passengers of the *Crowley*!"

Louis was stunned. The blood drained from Wragg's face.

"Commodore, I implore you, please give them more time," Wragg begged. "The lives of fifty innocents are at stake. Some misfortune must have befallen Marks and your men. Or perhaps they need more time to gather all the supplies. Surely, it can't hurt to extend the deadline another day."

"I have made up my mind. Death to all!" the pirate bellowed.

Louis felt sick to his stomach. *But they did nothing wrong. It's all my fault. I wish I hadn't suggested ransoming those poor people for medicine. Now they're all going to die because of me.*

When the prisoners learned they would soon be executed, they screamed and howled in despair. Their cries for mercy tore at Louis's heart. *I can't stand by and do nothing.* He needed to figure out a way to buy them more time. *I'll probably get flogged to death, but here goes.* He took two deep breaths and walked up to Blackbeard.

"Begging your pardon, Commodore, but are you sure hanging the prisoners is in your best interests?" As soon as the words tumbled out of his mouth, Louis knew he should have kept quiet.

Blackbeard glared at him. "*What*?" he hissed. "You have the nerve to question me?"

No sense holding back now. You're probably dead anyway. "My concern is solely for you, sir. Killing all those people means you'll be the most hunted man in all the seas. The entire British armada will . . ."

"Silence! You have no stomach, no spine. You are nothing but a lowly woodworm!"

Blackbeard was reaching for his cutlass when a pirate atop the crow's nest hollered, "They're coming! I see their rowboat riding low in the water! Looks like they're carrying a heavy chest."

Before the lookout finished his report, Louis fled into the hold and remained out of sight of Blackbeard for the rest of the day. Louis soon learned that on the foursome's way to Charleston, their rowboat had capsized during a violent squall. They clung to the overturned hull through the night and into the next morning, until they were rescued by a passing fishing boat. Once they reached the governor, it took longer than expected to find all the medicines on the list.

Louis heard applause and cheers coming from the *Crowley* after the prisoners were told they were free to go. He felt their relief and shared their joy. *Blackbeard was probably bluffing about hanging them,* Louis thought. *He wouldn't really have carried out his threat.* Louis would never know, but that's what he wanted to believe.

The next day, George Matson rushed over to Louis. George was the cabin boy for Major Stede Bonnet, a captain of one of Blackbeard's ships. "Did you hear the news, Louis?" George asked excitedly. "The king of England is offering pardons through the colonies' governors to anyone who gives up pirating. Blackbeard is planning to disband the fleet and accept a pardon from the governor of North Carolina. All his ships are meeting in Bath to divvy up the booty and get our pardons." Bath, the first town founded in North Carolina 13 years earlier, was located up the Pamlico River. "I've got to run. I'll see you in Bath next week. I can't wait to spend my share."

"Me, neither," said Louis, looking forward to getting his portion of the booty.

While some of the ships in his fleet left early, the remainder — the *QAR,* the *Adventure,* the *Revenge,* and a single-masted ship known as a sloop — headed north a few days later. On the way, Blackbeard made a surprise announcement that they would first go to Topsail Inlet in North Carolina to clean his flagship. When they neared the coast, Blackbeard — who was a master seaman — astonished his crew by ramming the *QAR* straight into a sandbar off a barrier island until she was hopelessly stuck. He beckoned the *Adventure* to come to his assistance and help free the vessel but, incredibly, she also became utterly wedged in the same bar.

The sloop and the *Revenge* anchored a safe distance away. Fearing the two grounded ships would break up in heavy surf, Blackbeard ordered all the stolen gold, silver, and jewels taken off the *QAR* and put on the sloop.

The crewmen spent the night on the sandy beach. The next morning, Louis, an early riser, woke up. As he stretched and yawned, he glanced at the dawn-lit ocean. *Something isn't right*, he thought. *No, this can't be!* He raced up and down the beach. The two grounded ships were tilted on their sides, and the *Revenge* was still anchored offshore. But the sloop was gone. He looked behind him and counted only 16 men. All the other pirates were gone, too.

"We've been marooned!" he shouted. "We've been left behind!"

As the others staggered to their feet and realized what had happened, they yelled in anger. "That slimy bilge rat," spat a pirate. "Blackbeard ran those ships aground on purpose. That was no accident. He had this all planned ahead of time. Once the booty was put on the sloop, he and his favorite men slipped away during the night. They wanted to keep all the booty for themselves and cheat us."

Louis went numb. "What are we going to do now?" The island on which they were stranded was more than a mile offshore, and had virtually no grass, trees, or fresh water. They had no rowboat. The *Revenge* was still anchored, but it was about a half mile away.

Later that morning, a storm blew in that prevented them

from swimming out to the *Revenge*. In fact, the surf remained rough for two days. With no food or water, the men were getting desperate. But then a ship appeared on the horizon and soon anchored nearby. The men recognized the ship as the one captained by Major Bonnet.

"We're going to be rescued!" Louis shouted with relief.

After the marooned sailors were brought on board, George Matson told Louis, "Major Bonnet went to Bath. When Blackbeard didn't show up, the major went looking for him and found you cast-offs. Bonnet is furious that Blackbeard double-crossed him, and he plans to hunt him down."

Bonnet reclaimed the *Revenge*, and the rescued seamen sailed with him to St. Thomas in the Virgin Islands where he sought a bigger crew. But Louis wasn't interested in pirates, pardons, or revenge anymore. "I'm sadder but wiser now," he told George. "The pirate life is not for me."

No one knows what happened to Louis Arnot, who, during his time aboard the Queen Anne's Revenge, *witnessed the taking of 18 ships.*

After being cheated by Blackbeard, Major Stede Bonnet continued to plunder other vessels while searching for Blackbeard but never found him. On September 27, 1718, Bonnet was captured by the British Royal Navy in a fierce battle near Cape Fear, North Carolina. He was tried and convicted of piracy and hanged on December 10.

Blackbeard — whose real name was Edward Teach of Bristol, England — kept up his pirating ways off the Carolina coast until he was killed on November 22, 1718, in a battle with British naval authorities near Ocracoke Inlet in North Carolina. Blackbeard was such a strong fighter that he was cut by swords 20 times and shot five times before he died. During his reign of terror from 1713 to 1718, he captured and plundered 40 ships.

In 1996, researchers off the Beaufort Inlet (formerly known as Topsail Inlet) in North Carolina discovered the remains of what is believed to be the Queen Anne's Revenge — the flagship of the most notorious pirate of his time.

THE LITTLEST
PIRATE

JOHN KING, CABIN BOY FOR
PIRATE BLACK SAM BELLAMY

John King sat glumly at the bow of the sailing ship *Bonetta*, staring out at the sun-speckled waves of the Caribbean. It was a picture-perfect day, but the 11-year-old boy was miserable.

He closed his eyes and wished he were nine again, when he was cruising these same sparkling blue waters with his father, the captain of a merchant ship. John loved his dad's thrilling stories of pirates and other seamen's tales. *Why can't it be the way it was?* he thought.

"Yo, John, your mother wants you!" crewman Kumar Patel shouted.

John ignored the sailor, even after Kumar hailed him several times. "Hey, boy, are you deaf?" Kumar asked when he reached John.

John shrugged and mumbled, "I wish. Then I wouldn't have to listen to *her*."

"What's wrong with you, boy? You've been moping for days."

John faced Kumar, a middle-aged sailor from India, and

poured out his heart. "My father died about a year ago — lost at sea during a hurricane — and now my mother is marrying some bigwig plantation owner in Jamaica. I can't stand him. He's an English fuddy-duddy with his nose stuck up. Ever since Father died and left us some money, Mother has been putting on airs like she's high society. And she's trying to turn me into the 'perfect little gentleman,' telling me how to do this and that."

"Aye, boy, that she is. Look at you. You're dressed like a young dandy in your fine silk shirt, knee britches, fancy buckled shoes, and silk stockings."

"Jonathon Meriwether King, get over here right now!" John's mother shouted from the main deck.

Her shrill voice grated on John. Every time he heard it, he told himself he would one day run away from his controlling mother. "I'd better go," he told Kumar. "It's probably time for my etiquette lesson."

Later, while his mother was teaching him the proper way to sip tea, John heard a commotion on deck. Kumar rushed down into their quarters and urged, "Hide! We're being boarded by pirates!"

John's mother began screaming. "They're going to molest us and then kill us!"

"Pardon me for saying this, madam, but shut up," Kumar said. "They won't hurt us, because we surrendered without a fight. They'll take what they want and then go on their way."

"But my clothes! My china! My silver!" she wailed.

"Say good-bye to them, madam."

"Pirates!" exclaimed John. "I've got to see them."

His mother grabbed him by the arm. "You will do no such thing," she commanded. "You will stay here and hide with me."

John broke free from her grasp. "You hide, Mother. I'm going to see for myself."

"I forbid you!" As he reached the door, she ordered, "Jonathon Meriwether King, get over here right now!"

Ignoring her, John dashed up onto the deck and skidded to a stop right in front of a tall, dashing man in his late twenties. He was wearing a blue velvet coat, black knee breeches, silk stockings, and silver-buckled shoes. Unlike many men of power who wore powdered wigs back then — it was November 1716 — he kept his thick black hair pulled back into a ponytail tied with a black satin bow. A sword swayed from his left hip, and four pistols stuck out from a red sash draped across his chest.

"Are you a real pirate?" John asked him.

The man glared at the brown-haired, freckle-faced boy whose hazel eyes were as wide as portholes. A hint of a smile crossed the man's lips. "I consider myself more of a Robin Hood of the Sea. I rob from the rich and spread the wealth around to my crew and me. And who might you be?"

"Jonathon Meriwether King from Antigua. I'm glad to meet your acquaintance, Captain . . ."

"Samuel Bellamy."

John's eyes grew even wider. "Black Sam Bellamy? The one they call the Prince of Pirates?"

Bellamy bowed slightly. "Excuse me, young man, I have business to attend to."

John rushed to the railing and saw that Black Sam's ship, the *Marianne*, was flying a black flag from her top mast and had her cannons trained on the *Bonetta*. With their weapons drawn, the pirates had scurried aboard and were giving orders in a relatively civil manner to the *Bonetta*'s 80-man crew. There was some pushing and shoving and the uttering of a few threats, but there were no major skirmishes.

This wasn't a hit-and-run operation. The pirates took their time, spending two full weeks methodically searching every inch of the *Bonetta* from bow to stern. They took whatever they wanted — including the Kings' furniture — and robbed each passenger and crewman of their jewelry and money. For those who complained, such as John's mother, the pirates showed little patience. "Look, we can do this the nice, easy way by you handing over all your jewelry, or we can do it the hard way," one pirate told her, pressing his dagger under her trembling chin.

Whenever the pirates carted off one of her possessions, she would scream in that irritating shrill voice of hers, "Oh, not that! It's my favorite! Take something else!"

Meanwhile, John found it all rather exciting as he perched on the poop deck, watching the pirates load the stolen goods onto their ship. The best part for him was talking to real pirates.

One of them was John Julian, a half-blood Miskito from Central America who joined Bellamy when the English captain had turned pirate a year earlier. "On land, my skin made me a nobody," Julian told John. "Here on water, I am a somebody. I am a good sailor, and maybe one day I will pilot a ship."

"But you're colored," said John.

"That I am. However, everyone is treated the same on Bellamy's boat — English, Dutch, Spanish, Indian, Swedish,

French, and African. It makes no difference. Look at the color of the pirates. How many are dark like me?"

John did a quick count among the 150 pirates. "I guess about forty."

"Most of them were former slaves," said Julian. "We would raid slave ships and offer some of the slaves a choice: Join us or get sold somewhere in the West Indies. It wasn't a hard decision for many to make."

Another pirate, Joseph Rivers, boasted to John that in just one year of raiding, Bellamy and his crew had plundered nearly 50 ships in the Caribbean and Atlantic. "We're getting rich quick, laddie," said the grizzled seaman, the oldest on board. "We might have been born to poverty, but we're going to die wealthy."

"What if you're caught today, tomorrow, or next week?"

"So we die," he replied. "Laddie, few of us have families or even homes. We have no countries to call our own. It doesn't matter what part of the world a man lives or how long he lives. What matters is that he lives well while he's alive."

To young John, living well didn't necessarily mean growing up wealthy. And it certainly didn't mean living in the prim and proper world of his dominating mother and his conceited, soon-to-be stepfather. *Someday I want to be free like the pirates,* he told himself. *I'm just a kid now, but someday . . . someday . . .*

When the pirates had finished their plundering, Bellamy called the *Bonetta*'s crew and passengers together and asked them, "Who wants to join me?"

"I'm tired of working on other people's jewelry," said one of the passengers, a goldsmith named Paul Williams. "I want to have my own gold." He stepped forward.

Right behind him was William Osbourne, a gunner's mate on the *Bonetta*. "The bad food on this boat can't be any worse than the "belly timber" you're offering. And at least I have a chance of making some money. I'm going with you."

Four other sailors and the captain's personal slave joined Osbourne and Williams, who were standing beside Bellamy.

I wish I was one of them, thought John. Then it struck him. *Why can't I be? When am I ever going to get a better chance to leave Mother? I don't want to live in Jamaica. Why not leave now?* From the front of the assembled group, John raised his hand. He tried to make his voice sound deep and adultlike, but it came out somewhat cracked when he shouted, "I want to go with you, Captain Bellamy!"

When the laughter died down, Black Sam chuckled and asked, "Aren't you a wee bit young?"

"No, sir. I'm strong for my age and I've learned things about sailing from my father — except he's dead — and I know I can have a better life with you than with . . ."

"Jonathon Meriwether King, hush up right now!" his mother shrieked. "You don't know what you're saying."

He wheeled around and said, "Mother, I'm old enough to make my own choices. I choose to go with Captain Bellamy — if he'll take me."

Her face grew red, and her hands flew in fury. "The captain is not going to take a boy like you. It's a *pirate* ship. You could never fit in among those ruffians. What kind of life is that? Stealing from the innocent, attacking the defenseless? Now quit this foolishness immediately. You're embarrassing yourself and me."

"Lad, perhaps you should listen to your mother," said Bellamy, amused by the boy's desire to turn pirate. "A pirate's life doesn't suit a child, especially one whose hands are soft and eyes are pure."

"Captain, have you ever wanted something so bad that nothing else matters?" asked John. "Well, that's how I feel. I want to go with you. I don't want to live a dull, boring life in Jamaica with my mother and stepfather. I just can't."

"Jonathon," barked his mother. "Stop this nonsense right now. You're bringing shame upon you." Addressing Bellamy, she said, "He isn't in the right frame of mind. He's been under enormous pressure — all of us passengers have — from your despicable, unrelenting siege."

Bellamy's stare locked on John's eyes. "I like your spirit, lad. I guess we could use another cabin boy."

Like getting whacked from a rogue wave, John's body went into shock for a brief moment. *It's really going to happen!* When he finally could speak, he squeaked out, "I'll get my things." He threaded his way through the crowd.

"You can't be serious," his frantic mother said to Bellamy.

"Madam, the boy is obviously unhappy and has nothing to look forward to but a prissy life with you and your new husband. At least on my ship, he can become a man."

"What kind of a man? A pirate like you?"

"He'll learn to be his own man."

"You've taken all my worldly possessions, and now you want to take my son?"

"It's his choice. I don't have the heart to say no to him."

When John returned with a bag of his clothes, he gave his

mother a quick kiss on the cheek and said, "Good-bye, Mother. Have a good life. I know I will."

The last thing he heard as the *Marianne* sailed away was his mother screaming, "John, come back!"

Over the next few days, John wondered if he had made the right decision. His mind was clouded by doubts. Conditions were a whole lot different than what he had ever been used to. The seamen's quarters below deck were cramped, smelly, and crammed with water casks, barrels of salted meat, coiled ropes, extra sails, supplies, and the spoils of plundered ships. The men slept in hammocks in shifts because they couldn't all fit in the space. The ship's head (toilet) was nothing but a plank with a hole in it extending out from the bow. There was absolutely no privacy. And the swearing! He heard words that he didn't know existed.

Throughout the Caribbean and the Gulf of Mexico, the *Marianne* continued to plunder ships, sometimes after a brief battle. John learned how to make hand grenades. He would take a hollow, baseball-size iron sphere, fill it with gunpowder, and plug it shut with a fuse sticking out. During battle, a pirate would light the grenade moments before he tossed it onto the deck of the enemy. John also helped supply the pirates with ammunition — birdshot and musketballs.

In February 1717, the *Marianne* and a second ship the crew had taken, the *Sultana*, were sailing between the islands of Cuba and Haiti when they spotted the *Whydah*, a beautiful three-masted, 18-gun, 100-foot-long English slave galley. Determined to capture her, Bellamy began stalking her.

"Why does the captain want a slave ship?" John asked Rivers.

"Judging from the direction she's going, this one could be a treasure ship."

"How can you tell?"

"Here's how it works, matey. It's like a triangle. First, the slave ship brings cloth, liquor, hand tools, and small arms from England to West Africa, the first part of the triangle. They trade the goods for hundreds of slaves and bring them here to the West Indies, the second point of the triangle. The slaves are traded for gold, silver, and sugar, which are brought back to England for a huge profit, the triangle's last point. The *Whydah* is heading north, which means she's probably loaded with riches."

For three days, the *Marianne* and *Sultana* chased the *Whydah* before they closed in on their prey and boxed her in. When the *Whydah*'s captain, Lawrence Prince, saw that he was outnumbered, he finally surrendered.

The pirates swarmed over their prize and whooped and hollered when they discovered the riches she held — gold and silver worth tens of thousands of dollars. Never mind that it came from the sale of innocent African slaves. Bellamy ordered his men to transfer the booty they had collected from their many previous raids onto the *Whydah*, which he made his new flagship. It was an astonishing fortune: nearly four and a half tons of silver, gold, gold dust, 20 tons of ivory, and "enough precious jewels to ransom a princess," Rivers told John. In all, the booty was worth an estimated three million dollars. For an honest sailor, who might have earned about 10 dollars a month, it was a fortune beyond belief. Even John, who was born into wealth, was overwhelmed.

Bellamy and the crew, which now numbered 180 men, divvied up the spoils and stored their treasure in chests below the ship's deck. John received a small pouch of silver, a one-quarter share, for his three months as an assistant cabin boy.

After Bellamy left the *Marianne* and took command of the *Whydah*, his cabin boys, including John, went with him. The pirate gave the slaver's former captain and crew possession of the *Sultana* so they could proceed to England poorer but unharmed.

Bellamy added 10 more cannons to the *Whydah*, converting her from a slave ship to a 28-gun pirate ship. Then, accompanied by the *Marianne*, the *Whydah* began the voyage toward the American colonies.

The first day of the cruise, John heard someone at the helm whistling a catchy tune. He recognized the whistler. It was John Julian, the half-blood Miskito. "I told you one day I would pilot a ship," Julian told the boy. "See? Anything is possible with Black Sam."

"Maybe when I grow up, I'll be at the helm of a pirate ship," said John.

As the two ships headed up Florida's east coast, the pirates couldn't help themselves. They continued to raid — and in some cases, take — vessels along the way. Bellamy doubled the size of his fleet with the addition of two captured vessels, the *Anne* and the *Fisher*.

When the captain of another captured ship was brought

aboard, Bellamy, as usual, had him escorted into his cabin, where John served them drinks. The captain, a wealthy English merchant, was outraged by the raid and angrily knocked the goblet of wine out of John's hand.

As the boy cleaned up the mess, the captain boldly scolded Bellamy. "I know what you've done in the Caribbean, Black Sam. How much plunder do you need? When is enough, enough? Prince of Pirates. Bosh, I say! You are no different than a low-life thief." He spat on the floor.

Bellamy glowered at him, but kept his composure, saying, "I am a free prince and I have as much authority to make war on the whole world as anyone who has a hundred ships at sea and an army of one hundred thousand men in the field. There is only one difference between you and me. Powerful people like you rob from the poor under the protection of the law. Pirates like me rob from the rich under the protection of our own courage."

Bellamy then had the captain's ship burned to the waterline and marooned the captured crew on a desolate Florida beach.

In the evening of April 26, the weather turned nasty and cold as Bellamy's fleet neared Cape Cod off the coast of Massachusetts. Gusts whistled through the ship's rigging. The sea began churning. Driving rain pelted the crew.

"We're caught in a nor'easter!" Julian yelled. The howling wind tore into the sails and swelled the waves into mountains. John had never experienced a storm as frightening as this. He was slammed from one end of the cabin to the other as the ship rose on the crest of a wave and then dived into the trough while rolling hard from starboard (right) to port (left). *This is scary*, he thought. *I hope the ship can weather the storm.*

The boy climbed into a large, nailed-down box of Bellamy's bedding and curled up in a ball. Gushes of cold water crashed through the windows, soaking the box. Above the roar of the pounding waves and the howling gale, John heard men shouting, praying, and cursing. He heard Bellamy order Julian to steer the *Whydah* out to deeper water. And he heard the horrifying screams of men who were swept overboard.

I wish I hadn't turned pirate.

The ship pitched violently port and starboard, her prow repeatedly pushed under the waves so deeply that the rudder kept lifting out of the water. So much seawater spilled down the tilting decks that the ship became heavier and harder to steer.

I'm going to die. We're all going to drown.

The waves, driven by gusts of up to 70 miles an hour, soared a terrifying 30 to 40 feet high before smashing into the *Whydah*, driving the ship ever closer to the dangerous rocks off the village of Wellfleet. There was no escape. Trapped in the surf, the vessel spun around and then slammed stern first into a sandbar.

I don't want to die. I wonder if Father felt this scared.

The floor under John began to split open. He leaped out of the box and lunged for the door, but a wave poured into the room and shoved him against the wall. He heard the mainmast crack and snap off. Another giant wave slammed into the *Whydah*, rolling her onto her side. Cannons fell from their mounts, smashing through overturned decks. Cannonballs, barrels, and boxes plowed into crewmen. Screaming pirates were tossed into the raging surf as the ship's back broke, splitting her between the bow and stern, and spilling out all her treasure and the rest of the crew.

John tumbled into the thunderous waves and clawed desperately under the surface in the inky darkness. In the roiling surf, he couldn't tell up from down. He was running out of air fast, and the ferocious undercurrent wouldn't release him from its deadly grip. Unable to hold his breath anymore, John quit fighting and thought, *I wish I were in Jamaica.*

Of the 145 crewmen aboard the Whydah *that night, 143 drowned, including John King and Black Sam Bellamy. The* Marianne *ran aground, killing most of those onboard while the other two ships, the* Fisher *and the* Anne, *rode out the storm, although they were badly damaged.*

The two survivors aboard the Whydah *were John Julian and carpenter Thomas Davis. They, along with seven crewmen from the* Marianne, *were captured by authorities the day after the storm. Julian was sold into slavery. The remaining eight were brought to trial on piracy charges. Davis and another carpenter, Thomas South, were found not guilty because they had been forced to join the pirates, but the other six were convicted and hanged in Boston.*

The wreck lay undisturbed until 1984, when Barry Clifford, a Cape Cod native, located the Whydah's *remains using sonar. So far, Clifford has hauled up more than 100,000 artifacts — such* as pistols, coins, and cannons — which are displayed at the Expedition Whydah Sea-Lab and Learning Center in Provincetown, Massachusetts.

Among the articles recovered were a small designer-crafted shoe, a stocking of woven French silk, and a leg bone — all belonging to a child around 11 years old.

Based on the historical record, John King was the youngest person ever to turn into a pirate . . . and die a pirate.

OUTFOXING THE FOX

BENTO GASPAR,
SEAMAN FOR PIRATE HOWELL DAVIS

Bento Gaspar didn't plan on being a pirate. It just sort of happened.

Born to parents who were slaves on the Cape Verde island of Fogo off the coast of West Africa, Bento and his parents were owned by Miguel Sousa, a kind, easygoing Portuguese official. Mr. Sousa was especially fond of the African slave family because Bento's father had risked his life to save Mr. Sousa from drowning in heavy surf during a fierce storm.

Although the Gaspars technically were slaves, Mr. Sousa gave them extra spending money and the freedom to go anywhere on the island when their work was done. Because he had many business dealings with the British, he had the Gaspars learn English so they could be more helpful to his guests.

Throughout his early childhood, Bento yearned to leave the island and explore the world. He kept begging his parents to let him ask for Mr. Sousa's permission. Shortly after his fourteenth birthday in 1718, Bento approached the owner. The teen was overjoyed when Mr. Sousa granted freedom not only to the teen but also to his parents. Mr. Sousa even arranged for Bento to get a job as a cabin boy on a merchant ship heading to the Bahamas.

"I will probably never see you again," Mr. Sousa told him. "There's a good chance the Portuguese government will name me a governor of an island somewhere along the African coast."

"I'm very happy for you, sir," said Bento.

"I will miss you, and certainly that delicious punch you would make for my guests." Mr. Sousa reached in his pocket and handed Bento a special gold coin stamped with the Sousa family crest. "Here, take this for good luck."

"Thank you, sir, for everything. You've been so kind to my parents and me. I am forever in your debt."

After a bout of homesickness, Bento adapted easily to working on a sailing ship, where all the crew were treated as equals. When they reached the Bahamian island of New Providence, Bento quit his job when he learned the vessel was going to be turned into a slaver. There was no way he would work on a ship that would carry hundreds of kidnapped Africans.

He then joined the crew of the *Buck*, one of two merchant ships that planned to sail together to South America. However, near the Caribbean island of Martinique some of the crew plotted a mutiny. Bento wasn't surprised. Most of his mates were former pirates and privateers. "Are you in or are you out?" one of them asked Bento.

"Aw, leave him alone," said an older sailor. "He's just a wee, scared lad," he said in a sarcastic voice, rubbing Bento's coarse black hair.

The short but compact teen bristled at the insult. "I'm fourteen and I can be just as tough as any of you. I'm in."

The mastermind behind the mutiny was Howell Davis, a clever, fast-talking 28-year-old Welshman and experienced sailor with a magnetic personality. When the numbers were in his favor, he seized the captain and tied him up. The mutineers then hailed the other ship, the *Mumvil Trader*, and invited the sailors to join them in a pirating adventure. Many scrambled over to the *Buck*. Those who wanted no part of such a life were allowed to continue on their way aboard the *Mumvil Trader*.

After the ships parted, the 35 men aboard the *Buck* overwhelmingly voted Davis as their captain. He drew up and signed articles of agreement, which included a pledge that no pirate would harm anyone who surrendered. After everyone, including Bento, signed the articles, Davis told them, "Whosoever we meet, we will steal their valuables and share them among us poor until we ourselves are among the rich."

In Bento's mind, it would be repayment for being a slave, even though he had been treated well. *Why shouldn't I get my share?* he asked himself. *Besides, maybe I can make enough to buy some land for Mama and Papa.*

The seamen of the *Buck* hoisted a black canvas sheet as her pirate flag and hunted for prey. Their first victim was the *Céline*, a French ship of 12 guns, which they captured with relative ease and no bloodshed. While in the *Buck*'s crow's nest watching his mates plunder the *Céline*, Bento spotted another ship heading toward them. "Sail off the starboard side!" he shouted.

As she came nearer, he could see through the telescope that she was flying a French flag. Under threat of torture, the captured crew of the *Céline* admitted to Davis they were familiar with the other vessel. She was the *Barfleur*, carrying 24 cannons and 60 men — nearly twice the guns and men as the *Buck*.

"Let's attack her!" Davis proposed to his men.

The crewmembers balked at first. "But, Captain, she has more firepower and men than we do," said one of the pirates. Most of the others murmured their agreement. "It seems like a foolhardy thing to do." Bento nodded, thinking, *I don't like this idea at all.*

"Nonsense, men," Davis countered. "You need to think smart. She would make a great ship for us, and I know how to win her. Trust me, men, for I have a clever strategy that I am confident will succeed."

Is he out of his mind? Bento wondered. *This is terrible.* Bento knew that, as an African, his chances of remaining free were slim if he were captured. *They'll make me a slave again.*

While Bento shuddered in dread, Davis projected an air of coolness and ordered the *Buck* and the much slower *Céline* to chase the *Barfleur*. When Davis was in yelling distance of the enemy, he ordered Bento to raise the makeshift pirate flag.

The captain of the *Barfleur* shook his head at such audacity and hollered, "I am far superior in guns and men, so I command *you* to strike [surrender]."

"No, sir," Davis retorted. "*You* must strike. I am prepared to engage in battle with you — a battle in which you most certainly will fare the worse." Pointing to the *Céline*, he said, "You see, my consort is approaching off your port side, so you will have to fight both of us. If you choose such action, I warn you, sir, we will give you and your men no quarter [mercy]."

The *Barfleur*'s captain scoffed at Davis and fired a broadside, when every cannon on one side shot at the same time. Davis responded with cannon shots of his own. As the *Céline* drew near, she raised a piece of dirty linen as her pirate flag and fired several shots. Then, all the captive crewmen on the *Céline* appeared on deck in white shirts and began shouting and cursing at the French ship.

At first, Bento couldn't figure out what was happening. But once he did, he began to understand Davis's scheme. The captives had been ordered at gunpoint to pretend they were pirates in a fake show of force designed to intimidate the Frenchmen. The trickery worked to perfection.

Thinking he was now greatly outnumbered, the *Barfleur*'s captain surrendered without firing another shot. Within minutes, his crew was shackled while the pirates plundered the vessel of valuables, food, and gunpowder. Then Davis released the Frenchmen and allowed them to sail off in their ships.

When the *Barfleur*'s captain realized that he had been hoodwinked and that the *Céline* wasn't really a pirate ship, he screamed in anguish. He was so distraught that he tried to throw himself overboard but was tackled by his officers.

The *Buck* sailed after new prizes and found a Spanish sloop, which proved easy pickings a few days later. More success followed. The *Buck* doubled the size of her crew to 70 from captives who turned pirate. They also changed to a new flagship, mounted her with 26 cannons, and called her the *Saint James*. So far, piracy was good for Bento.

The ship sailed to Gambia, on the West African coast, because Davis wanted to attack a fort known as the Gambia

Castle. It supposedly held a large quantity of money from selling slaves. When Davis announced his plans to the pirates, many doubted him. "But, Captain, how are we going to storm the fort?" one seaman asked. "It has so many guns that we could never get near it."

"Men, you show so little faith in me," Davis complained. "I have a scheme that I guarantee will work with little blood spilled. Have I steered you wrong so far?"

"No," they said in unison.

"Then we will execute my plan to the letter and add to our wealth."

When the *Saint James* neared the castle, Davis ordered all his men belowdecks, except for the dozen needed to sail the vessel. "If the soldiers at the fort see few hands [crewmen], they won't be suspicious," he told the crew. "Let them think we're just another trading ship."

Davis then called for Bento and told him, "You will come with me to pay a visit to the governor."

"Me, sir?" Bento replied in surprise.

"Yes, I want you to act as my personal slave. But really you're going to be a spy. They won't suspect a young African. Do you think you are up to the task?"

"They made their money selling my people, right?"

"Yes, Bento. They're slavers."

"Then I am more than willing to do whatever you ask."

The *Saint James* cast anchor under the fort, well within range of its guns. Davis — dressed like a well-off merchant in red bell-bottom pants, yellow shirt, and a matching feather in a wide brim hat — went ashore with three officers, five seamen, and Bento. On the way, the captain instructed them on what to say if any soldiers questioned them. Bento was starting to sweat from nervousness. *What if I say something wrong? What if they discover we're pirates?*

On reaching land, the party was escorted by a squad of musketeers into the fort and welcomed warmly by the governor, an Englishman named Thomas Jordan. In a bald-faced lie, Davis told him, "We're from Liverpool and bound for the River Senegal to trade for gum and elephant tusks. We are willing to trade our iron and silver for slaves."

"Wonderful," Governor Jordan said, clapping his hands. "Oh, would you by chance have any European liquor on board?"

"We have some for our own use, but I will share it with you. In fact, my slave here, Bento, makes the most delicious punch ever to tingle one's taste buds."

"You are most generous," said the governor. "I insist that you and your officers dine with me tonight."

"As commander of the *Saint James,* it will be necessary for me to see if she is properly moored and to give my crew certain orders. My gentlemen can stay, and I will return before dinner and bring the liquor with me. Meanwhile, allow my servant to assist your staff."

While in the fort, Bento made a mental note of the positions of the cannons and the placement of the guards. He spotted a sentry standing near a guardhouse, where about 20 muskets were stacked in a corner. He also counted 10 pistols hanging on the walls of the governor's main hall.

Accompanied by six more pirates, Davis returned to the fort. Like the captain, each was armed with two pistols concealed under his clothes. The plan called for the pirates to deliver the cask of liquor and then excuse themselves. They were to enter the guardroom and start up a friendly conversation with the soldiers. When the pirates heard Davis's signal — a shot from his pistol out the governor's window — they were to bind up the soldiers and secure the weapons in the guardroom.

After Davis arrived at Governor Jordan's residence inside the fort, Bento prepared the punch and served everyone. As he handed a cup to Davis, Bento whispered, "I've been through the house and didn't see any guards inside. Only the cook and his slaves are here, and they aren't armed."

"Excellent," said Davis.

Smiling, the captain walked over to Jordan, put an arm around him, and said, "I have a surprise for you, my friend." Then Davis whipped out his pistol and pressed it against the governor's chest. "Do not make a sound, sir. You are a dead man unless you surrender the fort and all its riches."

Jordan was too shocked to speak, causing Davis to repeat the threat. "Please, don't hurt me," the governor gasped in fear. "I will do whatever you ask."

With his men guarding the governor at gunpoint, Davis fired his pistol out of the window. The other pirates who had been making small talk with the guards drew their guns and tied up and gagged the soldiers.

Bento pulled a piece of black canvas from under his shirt, ran outside, climbed to the top of the fort, and hoisted the pirate flag — the signal for two more longboats of pirates to storm the castle.

Within 30 minutes, the pirates had taken total control of

the fort — and they did it without anyone losing a single drop of blood, just as Davis had predicted.

Bento felt exhilarated. He did his part in punishing a British official who allowed slavery — and the teenager would share in the booty. *I wish I could do this to all the slave lords.*

The governor, still shaken by this brazen assault, took Davis to a chest hidden in a secret compartment in a wall of the master bedroom. Bento and several pirates crowded around as Davis broke open the trunk. *There could be treasure worth a fortune,* Bento thought. Davis slowly lifted the lid, peered inside, stood back, and said, "What's the meaning of this?"

"I'm sorry, Captain Davis," said the governor. "I had sent the bulk of my money to a bank in London last week. All I have in here is gold worth a few thousand."

Davis frowned, wheeled around, and ordered his men, "Tear this place apart and take everything of value."

Although Bento was disappointed the chest didn't contain more money, he felt good stealing from a man like the governor.

After loading the *Saint James* with the spoils, the pirates dismantled the fort's cannons and demolished its gun towers so no one could fire on them. Then they freed all the guards and left.

Following the capture and plunder of three more vessels with little resistance, the *Saint James* met her match — a Dutch slaver with 30 guns and 90 men. The two ships engaged in a fierce battle, firing broadsides at each other from one in the afternoon until nine the next morning, when the Dutchman finally surrendered. For the first time, Bento saw the terrible price that he and his fellow pirates paid. Nine lost their lives, and 20 were badly injured — including Bento. Shrapnel from an explosion tore into his calf and fractured a bone. He had to hobble around wearing a splint made from wood and rope. Robbing the rich didn't seem all that much fun anymore.

Upsetting as that was for Bento, what bothered him even more was realizing that Davis was no different than Governor Jordan. While Bento remained on the *Saint James*, Davis took command of the Dutch slaver and sold the hundreds of slaves who were in her hold. The captain then converted the slaver into his flagship by adding more guns and named her the *Rover*.

Shortly afterward, the *Saint James* sprung a leak, causing the transfer of her crew and booty to the *Rover*. By now, Bento was suffering from a bad infection from his wound that left him feverish and in pain. There was little medication left in the medicine chest because of all the casualties from the battle. Bento spent his days doing little else but bearing his misery in silence.

Davis decided to anchor near the Portuguese island of Principe, off the coast of West Africa. When he came within sight of the island's main fort, the captain hoisted an English flag. Portuguese officials went out in a sloop to determine if the *Rover* was a friend or foe. In his charming way, Davis lied to them, claiming he was an English man-of-war in search of pirates lurking off the African coast. The officials guided the *Rover* into the port where she anchored below the fort's guns.

The governor, not knowing Davis was really a pirate, welcomed the captain and his officers and offered to supply them with whatever they needed. Davis thanked him, and in another lie, promised him that the king of England would pay for all the supplies.

With the *Rover*'s medicine chest restocked, the ship's surgeon was able to treat Bento's infection. But the young pirate was too ill to help his mates clean and prepare the vessel for her next cruise. From the deck, he watched with curiosity when, on Davis's orders, the pirates captured and plundered a French vessel that had entered the harbor for supplies.

"Have you ever seen such bravado?" a seaman asked Bento. "No one is bolder than Davis. He plunders a ship right in front of the authorities and gets away with it."

"But how did he manage that?" asked Bento.

"The good captain convinced the governor that the French crew was trading with pirates. Here's the really good part: The goods that we took? Davis told the governor that they were originally stolen by pirates and sold to the French, so we had to seize them for the king. The captain's story was so believable that the governor commended Davis and is throwing a big reception tonight in his honor."

Bento shook his head, marveling at the captain's nerve. "Like him or not, the man has guts."

"Listen, lad, there's more. Davis isn't content to leave this place without collecting some of its riches. So he's come up with a new scheme: He plans to make the governor a present of silver plates in return for his kindness. The captain has invited Governor Sousa and the island's most important men to dine on board our ship. They're coming tomorrow night. Then we'll clap them all in irons until we get a large ransom from . . ."

"Wait," Bento interrupted. "Who did you say the governor is?"

"Sousa. Manuel or Marcel or . . ."

"Miguel?"

"Yeah, that's it. He took over the governorship a few months ago from what I understand. Much too nice for his own good."

Bento's brain was reeling. *Mr. Sousa is here! I've got to get off this boat and warn him of the trap. It's the least I can do after all he did for my family and me. But if I tell him the truth, he'll know I'm a pirate. Will he be so angry with me that he puts me in chains? Will he sell me as a slave? I have to take that chance. I can't stay on board this ship anymore. I'm not cut out to be a pirate.*

Bento now focused his attention on a plan to alert Sousa. *I can't steal a rowboat without the night watch seeing or hearing me. I could try to lower myself by a rope off the stern and then swim to shore. I just wish I knew how to swim. Even if I could, the splint on my bum leg would probably drag me under.*

In frustration, he kicked a water barrel with his good leg. The barrel wobbled. Bento's spirits suddenly perked up. He had an idea.

That evening he made a gallon of his famous rum punch — extra strong — and gave it to the men on watch. They eagerly guzzled it down. After midnight, both had fallen asleep at their posts. Then Bento wrapped a harness around the empty water barrel and carefully lowered it over the side, using a rope and pulley. Next, he slid down the rope and untied it after he draped himself stomach first over the floating barrel. Luckily, the tide was coming in, so he clung to the barrel and waited as it drifted to shore.

An hour later, he reached the beach and limped toward the governor's residence.

"Halt! Who goes there?" came a voice in the darkness.

"I am a former slave of Governor Sousa. I must warn him. He's in grave danger. There is a plot to kidnap him and . . ."

Two guards rushed Bento and threw him to the ground. Convinced he was nothing more than a runaway slave, they dragged him off to a holding cell in the jail. No amount of pleading could convince them that his outlandish story was true and deserved the governor's ear.

Shortly after dawn, Bento gazed out through the barred window of his cell, feeling hopeless, when he heard a familiar voice. *It's Sousa. He's getting ready for his morning ride*! "Governor Sousa! Governor Sousa!" he yelled. "It's me, Bento Gaspar! I must talk to you!"

A guard immediately burst into the cell and clamped his hand over Bento's mouth. In a final frantic effort to contact the governor, Bento threw the gold coin Sousa had given him. It flew out the barred window and landed at Sousa's feet.

The governor picked up the coin, studied it, and then raced into the jail. He embraced Bento warmly and uttered in total puzzlement, "What are you . . . how did you . . . why are you in here?"

After Bento confessed he was a pirate, he revealed the kidnapping plot against the governor. Sousa told him, "Somehow you make me extremely disappointed in you, yet at the same time, enormously grateful for warning me. Now then, Bento, I want you to come with me to my house, get out of those ratty, smelly clothes, take a bath and then stay put."

"What are you going to do about the captain?"

"Davis might think I'm an easy mark, but I will outfox the fox."

After he was cleaned up and in new clothes, Bento learned that, at the invitation of the governor, Davis and his four officers agreed to meet Sousa at his residence for afternoon refreshments. Following strict instructions from the governor, Bento remained in his room and began writing a letter to his parents, who were still living on Fogo.

As the time approached for the five guests to arrive at the residence, Bento looked out the window of his second-floor room. He saw them walking up the path. From his vantage point, he also spotted other figures. Portuguese soldiers — more than a dozen of them — were hiding behind the trees on both sides of the path, their guns aimed at the unsuspecting pirates. *An ambush!*

When the gunfire erupted, Bento closed his eyes. He had seen enough seamen killed during his year as a pirate. He didn't need to see five more.

Outraged over the deaths of their leader and their top officers, the remaining crewmen aboard the Rover *bombarded the fort. Then they sailed off and named as their new captain Bartholomew Roberts — who soon became known as the infamous Black Bart.*

Bento (whose real name has been lost to history) returned safely to his family on Fogo.

OUT OF TUNE

HENRY HAMM, MUSICIAN FOR PIRATE THOMAS ANSTIS

"Oh, hi derry, hey derry, ho derry down,
Give pirates their gold and nothing goes wrong,
So merry, so merry, so merry are we,
No matter who's laughing at pirates like me."

The change of fortune for Henry Hamm came so swiftly and unexpectedly that the 12-year-old had yet to accept his new fate. Here he was on a pirate ship playing his fiddle and singing a song for a bunch of drunken buccaneers.

Just a day earlier, he had been fiddling for honest sailors aboard the merchant ship *Thomas*. Captained by his uncle Peter Hamm, the vessel was on an eight-week summer voyage in 1720 from Rhode Island to the Caribbean. Henry had been having the time of his young life. But then in sight of the island of Dominico, the *Thomas* was captured by the infamous Bartholomew Roberts, otherwise known as Black Bart. No shots were fired because the 14-man crew surrendered immediately.

As swarms of pirates boarded the *Thomas*, Henry folded his slender frame behind a rolled-up sail on the deck near the stern.

But a pirate with a flame-red mustache found the boy, grabbed him by his curly straw-colored hair, and dragged him out. Seeing Henry clutch his fiddle and bow, the pirate asked, "Can you play the fiddle?"

Trembling, Henry nodded meekly.

"Then play a tune for us, you catgut scraper."

Henry's fingers were shaking so much he could hardly grip the instrument. *They might kill me if I play badly,* he thought. After a squeaky start, he let the bow dance across the strings. The pirates stopped their looting and began clapping to the music. Two of them did a little jig. When Henry finished, mustache man said, "Boy, you're coming with me."

Oh, no, fretted Henry. *I didn't play good enough. They're going to throw me overboard.*

He was escorted to Black Bart's flagship, the *Royal Fortune,* and brought directly to the notorious Welsh pirate in his cabin. The rogue captain wore a burgundy vest and red breeches, a red tricorn (a hat with the brim turned up on three sides) with a red feather. Several gold chains were draped around his neck, including one that held a diamond cross.

"Play for the captain, like you did for us," mustache man ordered.

Maybe they like my playing, Henry thought. *Maybe if I play really well, they'll be nice to Uncle Peter and me.* Across the strings, Henry's fingers darted and the bow zinged, bringing a smile to Black Bart. "Bravo, lad," beamed the captain. To mustache man, Black Bart said, "We'll keep him."

The quartermaster brought out a paper and asked Henry, "Can you read?"

Henry nodded.

"Good. Then sign these articles of agreement. They're our rules."

"I don't understand," Henry stammered.

"You're staying with us, lad. You're a member of Black Bart's fleet now. Sign the articles."

Henry's knees nearly buckled, and his stomach twisted into a pretzel. He wanted to yell "noooo!" as loudly as he could. He wanted Uncle Peter to rush in and rescue him. He wanted to be anywhere but here.

He glanced at the dozen or so articles. But the rules barely registered in his brain, because he was still reeling from his capture. He glossed over the rules about not playing cards for money, keeping pistols and knives clean, and candles out by eight P.M. However, his eyes stopped on one that read, "To desert the ship or quarters in battle is punishable with death or marooning." *Is this really happening to me — being forced to turn pirate?*

"You should pay special attention to the last article," said the quartermaster.

Henry read, "The musicians shall have rest on the sabbath day, but the other six days and nights, there shall be rest only by special favor."

Beginning to lose his patience, the quartermaster, using an insult, ordered, "Sign it, you skinny grommet."

Henry hesitated only because it took a few seconds to gain control of his shaky hand. Obediently, he scribbled his name.

"What about my uncle Peter and the rest of the crew?"

"Oh, don't worry about them." The quartermaster motioned

for Henry to look out the window. He saw his uncle and the sailors rowing away from the *Thomas* and toward shore six miles away in a longboat. "Uncle Peter!" he shouted. "Uncle Peter!"

Mustache man yanked him away from the window and hissed, "Another outburst and you'll be fiddling for the sharks."

Tears dribbled down Henry's face. He felt so helpless, so alone. *What's going to happen to me? Will I ever get home again?*

About two dozen pirates had moved over from the flagship to the *Thomas*, which was now commanded by English-bred pirate Thomas Anstis. The ship, her name changed to the *Good Fortune*, now had her own little band — Henry; drummer Will Youngblood, 18; flute player Michael Fitzpatrick, 22; and their leader, veteran seaman Jasper Thornton on squeezebox.

"Wipe your tears, matey," Jasper told Henry. "You're a pirate now. Get used to it."

"What's going to happen to my uncle and the others?"

Stroking his thin gray beard, the shirtless musician, who was wearing a lime-green scarf on his bald head, said, "Black Bart was kind to them. He spared their lives and let them row to shore. They'll find their way back home, eventually."

For the rest of the day, Henry wandered around the deck, still in a daze over how his life had capsized. Jasper gave the boy time to gather his wits. By the evening, he sat Henry down to explain his duties on the ship, which included singing, dancing, and telling off-color jokes in addition to making music.

"We play when anyone asks us to play — day or night,"

Jasper said. "We can never refuse them, especially the captain. We play when they're working and when they're fighting."

"What? You want me to play the fiddle when the pirates are attacking another ship? But why?"

"Music inspires them, motivates them, rouses them," Jasper explained. "You have to play loud and fast during battle. You would be amazed at how that can rattle the enemy. Music and the sounds of war can have a chilling effect on their willingness to fight. You'll see."

"I'd rather not."

And so Henry's life as a pirate musician began with a command performance the next day for Captain Anstis and several drunken pirates. Sitting on a barrel, Henry rasped his bow across the strings, creating a lively tune. A muscle-bound pirate jumped up, clicked his heels, and began dancing. A heavy-set older pirate whipped off his shirt, wrapped it around his waist to look like a dress and, with his hands on his hips, danced opposite the first pirate. The others burst out laughing and clapped as Henry played his fiddle.

A few days later, the *Good Fortune* was sailing behind the *Royal Fortune* as they chased after an armed ship. The pursuers each raised their black flag, which showed a pirate holding a dagger while standing on two skulls.

The prey refused to surrender and fired off two rounds from her stern.

"All hands on deck!" Anstis shouted. "Battle stations!"

While the pirates rushed to their positions, Henry, Jasper, Michael, and Will met under the foremast on the main deck. Henry could hear the stirring music coming from the *Royal*

Fortune's six-man band of two trumpeters, two drummers, a fiddler, and a squeezebox player. With her black pirate flag flying high, drums beating, and trumpets blaring, the flagship attacked the vessel, which kept firing back. The *Good Fortune* closed in on the other side of the enemy.

"Play loud, mates! Play your hearts out!" Jasper shouted. Henry, his heart pounding even faster than Will's drumming, worked his fiddle and watched in disbelief at the wild scene in front of him. *This is insane,* he thought. *I'm playing music while people are trying to kill one another.* Nevertheless, he sang a fight song with the others:

> *"Heart of oak are our ships,*
> *Jolly tars are our men.*
> *We always are ready,*
> *Steady, boys, steady,*
> *We'll fight and we'll conquer, again and again!"*

The four musicians played on and on over the thunder of cannons, the shouts of pirates, the whistling of flying shot, the screams of the wounded. Within an hour, though, the other ship surrendered. *Finally,* Henry thought. *I can quit fiddling.*

"Now let's break out our victory song!" Jasper ordered, motioning for the band to walk with him to the railing and play as the captured crew was rounded up. After looting the vessel, the pirates marooned the captives on a small island and burned the ship.

When not in battle, Henry and his fellow musicians played and sang sea shanties — chanting songs — as the seamen performed their daily chores. The rhythm of the songs served to match the movements of the men as they toiled at repetitive tasks. The shanties also eased the boredom and lightened the burden of hard work.

Henry hated when he was ordered to play while captives were being tortured. He learned to fiddle with his eyes closed, but he couldn't drown out the anguished squeals of the victims. The first time it happened was after the capture of a Dutch merchant ship. Anstis was convinced that the owner was hiding jewels, so the captain brought him aboard the *Good Fortune*.

"Men," said Captain Anstis. "This calls for a good sweating!"

The pirates eagerly placed lighted candles in a circle around the main mast. The owner, a bearded, overweight man in his forties, was shoved into the ring. The captain told Henry, "Fiddler, play something fast." To the ship owner, Anstis ordered, "Now start running around the mast and don't stop until you're ready to tell us where you've hidden the jewels. Oh, and one more thing. If you step outside the circle of candles, we will kill you."

Henry played a catchy tune while Anstis kept shouting, "Faster! Faster!" Henry didn't know if the captain was referring to him or the poor man running in circles. By now a group of pirates had closed in on the ring and began jabbing and poking the sweaty, frightened man with forks and knives. Around and around he went until he began to stagger from dizziness, exhaustion, and the pain from dozens of cuts.

"I have ... nothing more ... to give you," he muttered, trying to catch his voice.

"I understand," said Anstis. "You must be extremely hot and thirsty."

The man, on all fours and breathing heavily, nodded. Henry noticed the man had a look of hope that the worst was over.

"Men," Anstis said, "cool off the poor gentleman and refresh him with water."

The pirates picked up the owner and, with glee, tossed him overboard.

The *Royal Fortune* and the *Good Fortune* continued to capture, plunder, and often burn raided vessels. But Henry began hearing complaints from the crew, because most of the spoils were ammunition, food, and rum; not jewels and gold. The pirates were getting well stocked, but they weren't getting rich.

Anstis and the crew weren't happy when Bartholomew Roberts ordered them to follow him to Africa. "Something big is going to happen," Jasper told Henry after the two ships anchored off the coast of Guinea in April 1721. "I don't know what it is, but be prepared for anything. Anstis and Roberts aren't seeing eye-to-eye lately."

The men on the *Good Fortune* took a vote and gave their captain permission to do what he thought best. The next morning, Jasper woke up Henry and said, "I told you so."

"What?" asked the sleepy-eyed boy.

"Our ship sneaked off during the night. We've split from Roberts for good and are headed back to the Caribbean."

"So let me get this straight," said Henry. "We're pirates on a pirate ship pirated from a pirate? This life keeps getting stranger and stranger."

Over the next few months, the *Good Fortune* raided several ships, including one they kept, the *Morning Star.* They fitted the vessel with 32 cannons and increased the size of both crews to more than 100 by taking men from other captured vessels.

Now Anstis had the men, firepower, and provisions to wreak havoc on the Caribbean. But Henry sensed that many of the pirates didn't share the captain's ambition. Some of the older ones were getting weary, and the newer pirates — the ones who were forced to join — were getting discouraged. The rest of his mates were constantly squabbling among themselves.

Knowing that a crew divided against itself cannot function, Anstis called for a vote on what to do. Henry was thrilled when the vast majority voted to quit. "I'll be able to go back to Rhode Island and be with my family again," he told Jasper.

"Not so fast, boy," Jasper said. "When you're a pirate, you can't just quit and go your merry way. We've angered many people and many nations. If they catch any of us, they'll bring us to trial."

"But we're just musicians and forced to . . ."

"You'd have to prove it in court. But there might be a way out for all of us."

The crew unanimously voted to file a petition with the king of England for a pardon. When the petition was drawn up, Henry and the others signed it in a round robin. The names were written in a circle so that everyone from Captain Anstis to Henry the fiddler carried equal weight. That way, the government wouldn't necessarily know who the leader was.

The petition claimed that they had been "forced by Bartholomew Roberts and his wicked crew to enter into Piracy and serve as pirates, much against our will. And we, your loyal subjects, utterly hating that sinful way of living, did with an unanimous consent run away with no other intent than the hope of obtaining Your Majesty's most gracious pardon." They sought a safe return to their native country "without fear of being prosecuted by the victims, whose valuables were taken by Roberts and his pirates, during our forced confinement on his ships."

The petition was given to the captain of a merchant ship bound for England. The pirates then camped out on an uninhabited island near Cuba to wait for a response that they knew would take a long time.

To eat, they fished, caught turtles, and fetched fruit from the lush jungle. Months went by without a word from England, and the idle men were bored, but Henry and his fellow musicians weren't. To pass the time and handle the boredom, the music makers were in big demand, singing, dancing, and telling outrageous tales.

For more amusement, the pirates held silly, fake trials. The men took turns acting as the prosecutor, judge, defendant, or jury member. A "criminal" one day might end up being the "judge" the next. Everyone had a trial — even Henry.

Bones, an officer for the *Good Fortune*, was the judge when Henry was brought before him on charges of singing off-key. Bones draped a dirty canvas over his shoulders for a robe, wore a large pair of spectacles, and sat in the nook of a banyan tree.

"If it pleases Your Lordship and gentlemen of the jury," said the pirate Rafe Kingman, acting as the prosecutor, "here is a lad before you who is a sad dog. He can't carry a tune. I humbly hope Your Lordship will order him to be hanged so our ears are no longer assaulted by his tone-deaf singing."

The judge peered down at Henry and said, "Hear me, you lousy, pitiful dog. What have you to say for yourself? Guilty or not guilty?"

"Not guilty, Your Lordship."

"Then sing a song," demanded the prosecutor.

Henry cleared his throat and began to sing a typical sea shanty:

> *"There was a ship, she sailed to Spain,*
> *Oh, roll and go!*
> *There was a ship came home again,*
> *Oh, Tommy's on the topsail yard!*
>
> *What d'ye think was in her hold?*
> *Oh, roll and go!*
> *There were diamonds, there was gold.*
> *Oh, Tommy's on the topsail yard!"*

Jury members and spectators hooted and booed, many sticking their fingers in their ears to show what they thought of the boy's singing talents.

"That's it? That's your entire defense?" the judge asked him.

"Your Lordship, I never claimed to be a singer. I am a fiddler, and a darn good one, too. You pirates have forced me to sing, so if anybody is guilty of making bad music, it's all of you."

Henry was drowned out by a chorus of more good-natured boos.

"We've heard enough," said the judge. Turning to the jury, he asked, "Have you reached a verdict?"

"Guilty!" they all shouted.

"Hear me, you young rascal," the judge told Henry. "You must hang for two reasons: First, because it is not right that I should sit here as the judge and not have someone hanged. Second, you have a hanging look about you."

The pirates wrapped a rope around Henry's chest and hauled him up so he was dangling from a tree limb a few feet off the ground. For his sentence, he had to sing while "hanging" for one hour.

In August 1722 — after nine months of holding wacky trials, singing sea shanties, dancing to fiddle music, and fishing — the pirates received word from England. Henry, like the others, was looking forward to hearing good news, allowing them to go home without fear of punishment.

"The king of England has chosen not to grant us the favor of a pardon," Anstis announced to the groans of the men.

Henry was devastated. *No pardon? That can't be. It's so unfair. That means I'm not going home. I might never get home. Now what will happen?*

The majority of the crew voted — many reluctantly — to return to their pirating ways. Henry wasn't one of them, but he had to go with them because he was a crewmember. They set sail in search of new victims.

While the *Good Fortune* was anchored off the Grand Caymans, the lookout in the crow's nest hollered, "Sail! Two of them off the stern!"

Peering through his telescope, Anstis hollered, "They're men-of-war! Cut the cable. Set the sails!"

Henry scrambled to his feet and began playing a fast tune, hoping the seamen would work even faster. *If the men-of-war capture us, we'll all be thrown in prison*, he thought. The two ships were gaining on them.

The vessels were almost within gunshot of the *Good Fortune* when the wind died, so Anstis ordered the men to break out the long oars. With Will Youngblood pounding a beat on his drums, the pirates rowed for their lives. The ship eventually caught a breeze and sailed out of sight of the enemy, which had no oars.

Ever since that close a call, Henry had trouble sleeping, knowing the Royal Navy was hunting for them. *It's only a matter of time before they catch us*, he thought. Although their hearts didn't seem in it, the pirates continued to raid other ships because they had nothing to lose. Henry glumly fiddled, but without his usual zip.

After capturing the sloop *Endeavor* in September 1722, Anstis brought her 14 crewmen onboard, burned the ship, and forced them to sign articles of agreement. When Henry learned that the captives were from Rhode Island, he perked up. Here was his chance to connect with his past and maybe even learn news of his hometown, possibly of his family.

Henry immediately sought out the *Endeavor*'s captain, Richard Durfey, and told him all about his capture and sordid life with the pirates.

"I know your uncle quite well," said Durfey. "He made it

back to Providence. Your family has been praying for your safe return, but they don't know whether you're dead or alive."

"I might as well be dead if I can't get home."

Captain Durfey put his meaty hand on Henry's boney shoulder, looked him square in the eye, and said, "Don't worry, son, we'll find a way to get you home."

A few days later, the *Good Fortune* anchored off a small island in the Bay of Honduras for general cleaning. During the night, a sailor from the *Endeavor* woke Henry and whispered, "Come with me, quietly."

In the moonlight, Henry noticed that the pirates who were on watch had been bound and gagged. Following the crew from the *Endeavor*, who silently were lowering themselves by rope over the side of the *Good Fortune*, Henry slipped into the water and swam with the tide to shore. They hid in the jungle until morning. When a group of pirates rowed ashore for water, the *Endeavor* sailors seized them and tied them up.

After Anstis discovered what had happened, he sent in another boat manned by 30 pirates. But the sailors, armed with weapons taken from the pirates, fired enough rounds that the boat turned around and returned to the ship. The sailors released the pirates they had tied up and let them swim back to the ship. Luck was on Henry's side, because the *Good Fortune* spotted a potential prize, weighed anchor, and headed out.

With the seized rowboat, Henry and the sailors reached the coast of Honduras and took passage on a vessel bound for New England. He arrived in Providence, Rhode Island, in spring 1723 for a joyous and emotional reunion with his family.

Henry's only regret from his two-and-a-half-year ordeal

was that he had left behind on the *Good Fortune* the only possession he truly treasured — his fiddle.

A month after Henry escaped, Captain Thomas Anstis was killed by his own men who were fed up with pirating. Other crewmen from the Good Fortune *surrendered to authorities, were tried, convicted, and hanged on the island of Curaçao.*

A year earlier, Bartholomew "Black Bart" Roberts was killed off Africa's Cape Lopez in a gun battle with the British warship HMS Swallow. *The men from his large fleet were soon captured. After what was then the largest pirate trial of its time, 54 pirates were hanged, 37 were sent to prison, and 70 African pirates were sold into slavery.*

As for Henry Hamm, no charges were ever brought against him. And there is no evidence that he ever went to sea again.

CUT OFF FROM THE WORLD

PHILIP ASHTON JR.,
FORCED SEAMAN OF PIRATE NED LOW

January 22, 1725

My dearest Mother and Father: I fear that you think I am dead or, worse, that I am a pirate. I am neither, although I can understand why word might have reached you that I had joined those sea demons.

I don't know if I will ever see you again because of my dire circumstances, but I must take this opportunity to explain what has happened to me over the past two and a half years. I yearn for the day when I will embrace you in our house in Marblehead. But if Fate, which has not been kind to me, deems otherwise, I hope this letter will reach you so that you can learn the truth of my dreadful adventures.

On June 15, 1722, I was captaining the schooner *Milton*, working the waters off Cape Sable in Nova Scotia with several other fishing boats. My three crewmen and I noticed a ship had anchored nearby. Soon four seamen from the ship rowed over to my schooner and politely asked to come aboard. They were friendly sorts looking to share news, so I welcomed them.

Once they were on my boat, they drew cutlasses and pistols from under their shirts and threatened to kill my crew and me. "If you cause us no trouble, we will spare your lives," one of them said.

I said, "We're just young lads catching fish to bring back to our home in Massachusetts. We are harmless. What do you want from us?"

The pirate cocked his gun and said, "We want your boat and your souls."

We were taken aboard their ship *Mary*, and who should prove to be captain but none other than the notorious Ned Low. As you've heard, this ruthless killer often murders those who refuse to join him and scuttles their vessels after taking anything of value. Low handed me their articles of agreement and ordered me to sign them. I told him, "No, I can't. My conscience won't allow me to turn pirate." He insisted, but I pleaded that it was against my nature and my faith to engage in robbery. I told him, "Please, let us go so we can return to our parents. We can do you no harm. We are just boys from Marblehead. Take my boat and let us go free."

Low grew angry with me, and two pirates dragged me away and threw me in the hold. By that evening, the pirates had captured all the other fishermen in the fleet, about 30 of them, and their boats.

The next day, my crew and I were brought to Low, who again demanded we sign the articles. I am proud to say all four of us refused. But the captain turned purple and took out his rage on me. He aimed his pistol near my head and pulled the trigger. The bullet missed me by inches. That was his plan. He wanted to scare me and he was most effective because I believed I wasn't long for this world.

I was shoved in the hold, where several pirates tried to convince me to become one of them. They said there were 42 pirates, and they needed another 50. They tried to convince me that pirating brings wealth. I knew better.

When their efforts failed, I was escorted to the deck again where Low yelled, "You, dog! If you won't sign our articles and go along with me, I'll shoot you dead." I was sure he would. My body trembled and I could hardly breathe, knowing that the next second could be my last. And yet something compelled me to speak forthright. I said, "Captain, my life is in your hands. I mean you no disrespect, sir. But I simply cannot be a pirate. It is not in my nature or my heart. Please, sir, have mercy on me."

If slapping me in the face with the back of his hand — which is what he did — is mercy, I will accept it instead of being shot. He put his mouth so close to mine that his foul spittle splattered my face, and he cursed me and shouted, "You sniveling dog. You will go with me whether you like it or not!" He turned to one of his pirates and said, "Put his name in the log as joining the crew."

I was now officially a pirate, although I swear to you that it was against my consent and everything you had so lovingly taught me.

On the fourth day of my captivity, Low released most of the fishermen because they were married, and he wanted no crewmen with wives. My three crewmen and I, none older than 18, were among those forced to stay.

There was one good thing that happened that day. Two of my young fishermen — George Lamont and Larry Faber — escaped by pretending to go along with the pirates. They took a small boat to the shore, promising to get a pirate's dog that was howling for his master on board. But the boys ran off. I hope they made it back to Marblehead.

Dearest parents, I cannot begin to express how sick in my heart I was when the pirates' ship sailed out into the Atlantic while so many of my fellow fishermen had been set free. But before they left, the quartermaster Russell stabbed me not with his cutlass but with his words. He lied, telling the fishermen that I had turned pirate by choice. If they have passed on that lie, I pray you know I would never allow my morals to be poisoned by the pirates or share in their spoils.

When I lost sight of land, all hope of an escape was gone, and I wept bitterly. For days, I pleaded for my deliverance. On Low's orders, Russell thrashed me with the flat side of his sword, demanding I sign the articles of agreement, but still I refused. I expected every day would be my last.

But then I was given a wee bit of comfort from a pirate who told me, "You fret for nothing. The articles say we cannot draw blood or take the life of any man after we have given him quarter — unless he commits a crime." Although I was still abused after hearing that, I felt a little better, believing they wouldn't kill me after all.

Most anything short of death was preferable to being linked with such a vile crew of scoundrels who found it fun to rob people, abuse villagers, kidnap sailors, get drunk, and curse to their hearts' contempt.

At Carbonear, Newfoundland, I watched helplessly from the ship (which Low named the *Fancy*) as the pirates went ashore and pillaged the town of all that was worth value and destroyed the homes. My only relief from this sad episode was learning that the pirates did not hurt those poor people.

My awful life on the *Fancy* got worse when we were caught in a fierce hurricane. All hands were forced to work around the clock to save the ship. My instinct for survival overtook me. I confess, dear Mother and Father, that I worked with the pirates, so afraid was I that we would be swallowed up by the violent sea. Our only goal was to stay afloat among the tremendous waves, so it required that we toss much of their goods and provisions and six guns overboard. For five days and nights, the *Fancy* was battered from bow to stern.

During the height of the storm, I noticed these wretched pirates — who seem so fearless and daring under a clear sky or against helpless people — became sniveling cowards. I could plainly see the inward horror and anguish on their scarred faces and I heard them shout, "Oh, I wish I were home!"

But once the tempest ended and we all had survived, the pirates once again were cursing, swearing, drinking, and talking about their next battle.

We repaired the ship on a small Caribbean island. You'll notice I wrote "we." Yes, I confess I helped them, partly because I was ordered to work and partly because staying busy made the days go faster. Then we sailed toward Grenada, a French island in the Caribbean. We needed water desperately because we were down to a half a pint of water a man for 16 days.

Low knew that the French officials might suspect the *Fancy* was a pirate ship, so the captain ordered most of the crew to stay belowdecks. He fooled the officials into believing he was a merchant, so they let him replenish his water supply.

But a French pirate ship, the *Loire*, with her 30 hands and four cannons tried to take over the *Fancy*. When the *Loire* came alongside us, Low called up the 90 pirates hiding belowdecks. The Frenchmen realized too late that they were outnumbered and outsmarted, and they gave up without much of a struggle.

Low took over command of the *Loire*, giving the *Fancy*, which I was on, to his first mate, Francis Spriggs.

After this capture, the pirates cruised through the West Indies, raiding seven vessels, often resorting to disgusting brutality. The acts of needless violence and evil torture that I witnessed are simply too horrible for me to write about. I confess I had some involvement in the capture of these ships, but it was only to drag the dead and wounded away during the heat of battle.

In January 1723, I marked six months aboard the *Fancy*, never having felt the firmness of Mother Earth. We sailed near the island of Curaçao where I received a terrible scare. The British man-of-war *Mermaid* chased the two pirate ships. Spriggs's and Low's vessels sailed in opposite directions, but the *Mermaid* went after Spriggs and was catching up to us. I felt great terror because if we were captured, I would have been considered a pirate. I had no proof to the contrary, plus my name was on the crew roster, so surely I would have been hanged in disgrace.

Therefore, I was put in the uncomfortable position of rooting for the pirates and against the British crew — the very people who, if they knew the truth, would have been my saviors.

The *Mermaid* was closing in on us. But a pirate on board knew of a shoal where the water was deep enough for our ship to clear but not deep enough for the *Mermaid*, which had begun to fire on us. We sailed over the shoal and then watched the *Mermaid* run aground. The pirates cheered. All I could think about at that moment was that I was saved from a hanging.

The *Fancy* was alone with only 22 men aboard. Spriggs decided to head for New England and recruit more pirates. I thought this would be a great chance for me to escape. I found seven men who wanted to leave with me.

But Fate was cruel to me. Shortly after our ship reunited with Low's, a pirate overheard us plotting our escape and reported us to Spriggs. I had never seen him so angry. He yelled, "You dog, Ashton, deserve to be hanged from the yardarm for designing this scheme."

I replied, "I had no desire to hurt any man on board. I just want to get off of this ship and go about my life."

He said, "The matter is up to Captain Low whether you live or die."

I feared the worst, naturally. But I was lucky. For some reason, Low was in high spirits that day. When Spriggs told him of the plot, Low waved it off with a laugh and said, "Spriggs, if I were in Ashton's shoes, I would have tried the same thing."

Spriggs was furious and told me, "Make no mistake about it, young man. You are a pirate. You are on a pirate ship and you have helped us while we attack and plunder. If you are caught, you will face what all of us will face — the noose."

I will never forget what happened the next day, on March 9, 1723. The ships were anchored outside an uninhabited island in the Bay of Honduras. I was friendly with the cooper, the man in charge of maintaining the barrels. He and six hands in a longboat were getting ready to go ashore to fill casks with fresh water from a spring. I knew this was an opportunity I needed to seize.

I begged the cooper to let me go with him and help. He agreed, figuring there was no way I could escape. I certainly wouldn't be foolish enough to hide on a small island without any supplies. All I had on was a jacket, trousers, and cap. I had no shirt, shoes, or socks. Had I known earlier they were going to shore, I would have prepared myself by hiding on me a knife and other necessities. But I had to take the chance now.

Once I got on dry land, I was resolved that come what may, I would never step foot on that ship again. I gave the cooper and others no hint of my plan to escape. I helped get the casks out of the boat and rolled them up to the watering place. Then I gradually strolled west along the beach, picking up stones and shells, sneaking farther and farther away. The cooper spotted me and asked where I was going. I told him I was gathering some coconuts.

As soon as I got out of sight, I took off in a dead run to the north. Bushes and fronds slapped my face and scratched my arms. My bare feet were cut and bleeding, but I didn't care. All I thought about was escape. Deeper and deeper I ran in the jungle and then I did something I thought was clever. I headed east for a while and then south back toward the beach and hid in a thicket where I could hear them talking. I figured that if they went hunting for me, they would search the west side of the beach, while I was now hiding behind them on the east side.

After they had filled their casks and were ready to cast off, the cooper called after me. The other pirates shouted my name, too. But I remained silent. I heard one of the pirates say to the others, "The dog is lost in the woods and can't find his way out."

The cooper told them, "No. He has run away and won't come out. It's impossible to find him in this jungle." Then he cupped his hands and shouted, "Philip, I know you are trying to escape. But you will die on this island without provisions. You are better off coming with us. You have five minutes, and then we are leaving for good — and making note of your eventual death."

There was nothing he could have said that would have changed my mind. All I wanted was for them to leave and be out of my life forever. They waited five minutes and then they left. I crept out to a spot where I could see the two pirate ships and wondered if they would send a search party to find me. Much to my relief, I saw them weigh anchor and sail off.

Yes, I was on a desolate island. But to me the wilderness and loneliness made for far better company than anything I had found in nine months aboard the *Fancy*. My thoughts were not on how I planned to survive on this forsaken island; only that I was no longer part of those wicked pirates. When they were gone and the coast was clear, I leaped up and shouted for joy.

It wasn't long before my stomach growled. Quickly, my

happiness was doused by a harsh reality. I was stranded on an island alone. My only possessions were the clothes I was wearing. I had no knife or gun to hunt with. If I was lucky enough to catch an animal, I had no way of cutting it up. Even if I could cut it up, I had no way to cook it. I sat on a rock and wept until I was drained of all tears.

Then I dunked my head into the spring and told myself that I would find a way to survive. I would live off fruit and vegetables and build a shelter with my bare hands. I felt confident that a native would row by or that a ship would anchor for fresh water, and I would be rescued. I figured I would be stuck on the island for a week or two. How wrong I was!

I used a broken shell to mark each day with a notch on a palm tree. The days turned into weeks and the weeks into months. For the next nine months, I never saw another human being. The only living creatures, other than the insects, were snakes, wild boar, and birds. I survived on grapes, figs, plums, and on raw turtle eggs that I dug up on the beach. I used palm fronds to build a crude hut just big enough for me to lie down. The nights were the worst. I had no way to start a fire. The mosquitoes were so thick that I could barely open my mouth to eat without one of them flying inside. Sand fleas and tiny biting flies made sleeping on the beach impossible. The best way to escape the insects was to swim in the ocean, but there were always sharks in the shallow water.

Having no shoes, I was in constant pain, because my feet were torn to shreds from the sticks, rocks, and thorns of the jungle floor and the broken shells in the sand. I was always hungry and growing weak, sleeping much of the time.

Then one day in November, I saw an elderly native in a dugout canoe fishing nearby. I stumbled down to the beach and hailed him. It felt strange hearing my voice for the first time in nearly a year. The fisherman came to the beach. Because he spoke Spanish, which I didn't, the two of us could communicate only through gestures. His name was Rico. He was a friendly sort and figured out that I was either a castaway or a shipwreck victim in desperate need of help.

Rico had flint and a knife, and he built a roaring fire. Together we roasted fish that he had caught. Dear Mother, you know how much I love your cooking, but this was truly the best meal I had ever tasted. I savored every bite. It was especially tasty because I believed I would soon be leaving this island with him.

But, alas, Fate refused to release its grip on me. A few hours after Rico went out in his canoe to fish, a terrible storm lashed the island for nearly a day. He never returned. He probably capsized and drowned, and his death left me deeply saddened. The only good thing for me was that Rico had left behind a machete and flint, so I was able to hunt, stay warm, and cook food during the cold, rainy season.

I was pretty certain I would never see you, dear Mother and Father, ever again. I figured it was only a matter of time before I died here.

In June 1724, after 16 months on the island, I had grown so weak that I passed out on the beach. When I came to, I was shocked to find myself surrounded by 18 Englishmen. Once they convinced me they were real and not a figment of my imagination, I felt great joy. But my happiness was tempered by what they told me. They had been living on the island of Barbarat and had fled in their rowboats because Spanish pirates were about to attack. The English planned to stay on my island indefinitely for safety, so any thought that I might get home soon had vanished. At least they brought pistols and also tools, which we used to construct shelters with roofs of thatch and sticks for walls. We named our compound Castle of Comfort.

Compared to the bare existence that I was living before, this was luxury. I enjoyed cooked food, better shelter, and decent company. The leader was a kind soul known as Old Father Hope. He would lead us in prayer and song every night. But there were others in the group who reminded me too much of the pirates who had ruined my life.

About six months after the English arrived, four of us took a rowboat to a small nearby island to hunt for tortoise. After a successful day, we were returning at dusk when we heard an exchange of gunfire. Pirates in two longboats were attacking our people.

I wanted to help my English friends who were under siege, but the others in my boat insisted that even though we had firearms, we were no match for the invaders. We needed to save ourselves. We began rowing toward an uninhabited island about a mile away when an anchored pirate ship came into view.

The ship looked familiar, and it flew a black flag with a white skeleton. In one hand, it was holding an arrow piercing a bleeding heart and in the other hand, it was holding an hourglass. Dear Mother and Father, I cannot begin to describe the despair I felt at that moment, for it was then I realized the flag belonged to Captain Spriggs, and the ship was none other than the *Fancy*.

What were they doing there? Did they spot the English and want to raid their little settlement? Did they come for water? Did they return to hunt me down? I never found out because I was trying to flee for my life.

The pirates spotted us and gave chase in a longboat. As we neared the little island, we heard them shout, "Surrender now, and we will give you good quarter."

My friends in the boat paid them no heed. They were as terrified as I was, although I had more reason to fear the pirates. I knew that if I should fall into the hands of those scoundrels again, they would surely torture and kill me for deserting them.

We reached the beach about a minute before the pirates did and hid in the jungle. Thankfully, the pirates didn't chase after us. Instead, they shouted, "If you won't come with us, then you will die on this stinking island!"

My friends wanted to give up, but I convinced them to stay put. We watched the pirates take our boat, with all the food in it, and row back to the ship. We were stranded on the tiny island, unable to shoot game or build a fire for fear of giving away our position. We survived on fruit and rainwater for five days until the pirates left. The four of us figured we would have to swim the mile across shark-infested waters to get back to the Castle of Comfort, or what was left of it.

But great joy! Old Father Hope rowed out and rescued us. But then he described the terrible ordeal the Englishmen suffered: "The pirates had discovered our settlement, and they struck us and abused us. Thomas Grande turned pirate, and he told them where I had hid our valuables. They dug it up and then they beat me. When they left, they made us swear not to come to the island to rescue you."

The pirates were definitely Spriggs's people. Apparently, he and Low got into a quarrel a year earlier and split up. Spriggs's men bragged they had captured 40 vessels since then.

Now comes the reason for this letter to you, dear Mother and Father. After all that has happened, it is clear that Fate has more cruel jokes to play on me and that it is likely I will never get home. Old Father Hope gave me pen and paper so that I might set the record straight about my life, as awful as it has become since I was captured by pirates. My English friends promised that if I should die, they will do everything within their power to get this letter into your hands, assuming they ever get off this island. I will put this letter into a corked bottle so if anything happens to them, perhaps Fate will grant me one wish and allow someone to discover it and deliver it to you.

Please know that not a day goes by that I do not think of you, my dear parents. You will remain in my heart forever.

Your loving and faithful son,
Philip

In March 1725, a merchant ship from Salem, Massachusetts, anchored near the island where Philip was stranded. He rowed out to the vessel and was warmly received by the crew. He returned to Marblehead on May 1 — almost three years after pirates had captured him. When he saw his parents, "I was received as one coming to them from the dead, with all imaginable surprise and joy," he later wrote in a short memoir.

Philip's fellow fishermen made it safely back to Marblehead. Joseph Libbie, one of Philip's crewmembers, turned pirate, was captured by authorities and later hanged.

In 1724, Captain Ned Low was set adrift in a small boat after a mutiny by his crew. He was picked up by a French warship and hanged on the island of Martinique. Spriggs reportedly had plundered more than 50 ships before he disappeared.

TREASURE SEIZED, TREASURE LOST

LOUIS GARNERAY, SEAMAN FOR PRIVATEER JEAN-FRANÇOIS MALROUX

Louis Garneray was dozing on deck when a shout from above jarred him awake.

"Sail!" yelled the watchman from the ship's crow's nest. "Dead ahead!"

Like many of the crew aboard the armed French ship *Iphigénie*, Louis scrambled to the railing near the bow and gazed out across the gently rolling Indian Ocean. In the distance, the 16-year-old seaman spotted a large three-masted vessel. His heart started pounding. *Is it a merchant ship? An English man-of-war? A slaver?* No matter; chances were good that he and his crewmates would be locked in deadly combat with the other ship.

From the poop deck (the raised rear deck) Captain Jean-François Malroux stared in his telescope at the approaching vessel. Louis held his breath as he studied the captain's face, looking for a sign. Soon a grin crept across Malroux's lips. "Gentlemen!" he shouted to the crew that had gathered on the main deck. "She's the *Pearl*, the merchant ship we've been looking for, and she's flying English colors, so she's fair game. She sails low in the water, which means the booty is still in her hold. Gold, silver, and jewels — a fortune for each of us!"

Louis and the others erupted into wild cheering. He and his 129 shipmates were privateers — pirates who had government approval. Captain Malroux had a letter of marque from the French government granting his ship the right to attack English vessels and keep most of whatever the ships contained. This was 1799 — a time of war between the British and the French.

I'm going to be rich! thought Louis. *No longer will Papa worry that my head was swimming with mad ideas about a life at sea.*

Against the wishes of his family, Louis had left his home in Paris in 1796 and joined the French Navy at 13 — the minimum age to enlist as an apprentice seaman. But whatever romantic notions he had as a mariner were drowned the moment he stepped onto the deck of his first naval vessel, the *Forte.* Instead of sharp seamen and officers clad in crisp, clean uniforms, the ship was shabby and packed with dirty-looking sailors in tattered garments and bare feet. *They look more like pirates than seamen of the Republic,* Louis thought. *A beggar wouldn't wear their clothes.*

On his first voyage, Louis found the work hard, tough, and exhausting. His hands bled, his muscles ached, and his stomach craved a decent meal. But the boy, whose short, small-boned frame and curly brown hair made him look young for his age, was eager to learn.

For the next couple of years, the apprentice learned the

ropes of a mariner at war on board another French naval ship, the *Preneuse*. Although sailors for the French Navy put their life on the line, they didn't get paid unless they captured an enemy ship. If they did seize such a vessel, one-third of the value of the ship and her cargo went into a fund for retired or disabled seamen, one-third to the ship's officers, and one-third to the crew.

Despite his youth, Louis proved an able hand during sea battles. As enemy guns blasted his ship, he never hesitated to perform his duties. He scurried back and forth to deliver gunpowder to the gunners, pulled fallen crewmen away from the line of fire, and repaired rigging as bullets and shrapnel flew by him.

Several times the *Preneuse* traded cannon fire with English warships, but because she was so often outgunned, she usually fled. Then in September 1799, while encountering two English warships near Mauritius, an island in the Indian Ocean, the *Preneuse* sank under a barrage of deadly fire. Louis was rescued and made it safely to port.

By this time, he was through with the navy. In the three years that he had been an apprentice seaman, the teen had been battered by stormy seas, shot at by British warships, held dying crewmen in his arms, put out fires on board the ship, and suffered from strange, tropical illnesses. And for what? He had yet to receive one day's pay because neither ship that he was on ever captured an enemy vessel.

It was time to leave the navy and become a privateer. The French government gave privateers the full value of any prize they captured except for five percent, which went to a fund for wounded seamen. So Louis signed on with Captain Malroux, a French privateer and commander of the *Iphigénie*, a three-masted ship with 16 guns and a crew of 130.

Now, just days out on his first voyage as a privateer, Louis was poised to battle the merchant ship *Pearl* in a winner take-all clash that could make him rich. Or dead. He and his fellow shipmates didn't care that the *Pearl* carried 24 guns and had a large crew that was equally determined to fight to the death. This was a golden opportunity to strike it rich.

As the ships drew within range of each other, Captain Malroux spread the word for the crew to race up the rigging and crowd the rails as if they were getting ready to board the enemy vessel. But they were not to board until he gave the command. Once they took their positions, they yelled insults and threats to the *Pearl,* which responded by firing several cannon shots that fell short of the mark.

Standing at the railing, Louis saw that the *Pearl*'s decks were crammed with cutthroat sailors itching to fight. Trickles of sweat spawned by excitement and fear slithered down the teen's back.

"There are more of them than there are of us," he said to Duncan, the grizzled sailor next to him. (Many seamen used only one name.)

"Aye, but there's not a soul on board here who doubts that we can take her — unless you're the only one." Duncan studied Louis's face for a sign of weakness or cowardice.

There was none. Louis hid his fear well. "There's no doubt from me, mate," said Louis. "I'm more than ready." He gripped his musket tight around his sweaty fingers.

When the two ships were only a few yards apart, the *Pearl*'s crew abandoned their cannons without reloading and rushed to the rigging and railing, preparing to prevent the *Iphigénie*'s men from boarding. But Malroux tricked the enemy. The *Iphigénie* changed course for a better angle and then let loose her guns, blazing away with grape shot — small cast-iron balls wrapped in canvas that flew out like buckshot. Louis and his shipmates fired round after round while the cannons on the gun deck below thundered.

On the *Pearl*, wounded sailors screamed in agony and tumbled to the deck. Louis thought nothing about killing or wounding another human being. They were the enemy and they were shooting back. *It's either them or us*, he thought as he picked off sailors one at a time with his musket. For nearly an hour, the *Iphigénie*'s guns pounded the merchant ship, which was becoming increasingly powerless to fight back because so many of her own cannons had been destroyed.

"Keep firing!" Captain Malroux ordered. "Show no mercy, for they would surely want to murder us in the name of England!"

The smell of gunpowder was thick in the air when the *Pearl* finally lowered her flag in surrender to the boisterous cheers from the *Iphigénie*. Malroux ordered 30 men to board the *Pearl*, whose crew had lain down their arms and awaited their fate. They were put on longboats and taken to shore, where they couldn't pose any problems for the victors. Meanwhile, Louis and the rest of his shipmates spent the remainder of the day repairing what little damage was inflicted on their vessel.

Next, the crew transferred the valuable cargo from the

Pearl to the *Iphigénie*. For many, it was the happiest task of their lives. They had struck the mother lode — a treasure ship. Each chest of gold, each crate of silver, each container of precious stones that was hauled aboard the *Iphigénie* brought a hearty cheer from the merry sailors.

"I'm rich! Filthy rich!" bellowed Duncan.

"You mean you're *filthy* and rich!" Louis retorted.

Duncan picked up a bucket of water and dumped it over Louis's head. "And you're *wet* and rich!"

Louis laughed. He didn't mind being drenched on such an extraordinary day. "I love the sound of that word. Rich. Rich. Rich."

Everything was taken out of the *Pearl*'s hull except for the 50 fine Arabian horses onboard. They would fetch good money back in port.

By nightfall, the elated crew broke into song, guzzled rum, and danced on deck. It all seemed so unreal to Louis. Earlier that day, he was fighting in the midst of an intense, bloody sea battle where, if luck were bad or an enemy's aim good, grapeshot could have ended his life. Now here he was just hours later, resting against the base of a mast, watching his drunken shipmates celebrate their newfound wealth, and dreaming about his own.

Louis's brain fluttered with delightful thoughts of how to spend his share of the booty. *A cottage with a garden for Mama and Papa. Fancy clothes. My own apartment on the Seine.* He gave absolutely no thought to saving any of his capital.

Duncan nudged Louis and pointed to Captain Malroux. "Look at him, lad. He's the only one onboard who isn't happy."

Louis noticed that the captain seemed somber, almost sad — a reaction that would have made sense had the *Pearl*'s cargo hold been empty. "What's wrong with the captain?" Louis asked.

"He's a man always under a dark cloud, lad," Duncan responded. "I went up to congratulate him and he told me, 'Bad luck is sure to follow.'"

"Why would he say that?"

"Because bad luck *does* follow him wherever he goes. Mind you, he's as fine a mariner as has ever sailed the seven seas, but he's a cursed man. It seems that in every battle, he's the last one wounded. The last bullet fired, the last slash of the cutlass by the enemy always finds our captain."

"But, Duncan, he doesn't look wounded to me this time."

"Aye, and that's what's troubling him so. Too many good things have happened today. He's waiting for the bad luck to crash down on him like a snapped foremast in a heavy storm."

With a calm sea and a good wind, the joyful young privateer, like the rest of his shipmates (other than the captain), had no worries over the next few days. Their ship and the *Pearl*, which was manned by a skeleton crew from the *Iphigénie*, headed victoriously toward their home port in Mauritius. *Life is good, very good*, thought Louis. *And I'm rich!*

When dawn broke five days later, the crew spotted two ships bearing down on them. By twilight, the vessels were close enough for the crew to identify them as British ships — the *Trincomalee*, a big three-masted vessel with 22 cannons, and the *Comet*, a smaller schooner with four cannons. Judging from the way they were maneuvering toward the *Iphigénie* and the *Pearl*, it was obvious they weren't planning a social visit.

From the poop deck, Captain Malroux addressed his crew. "Ill fortune still has a firm grip on my fate to which you, my friends, regrettably are attached. While all of you basked in good luck, I was feeling the hot breath of doom on my neck. I had reason, as you can plainly see now. There is no doubt that we are about to be attacked. We cannot outrun them."

Louis's heart sank. *No! No one is going to take away my hard-earned booty. Not without a fight.*

Malroux unexpectedly changed his tone from one of gloom to one of resolve. "Gentlemen, we are far from defeated." His men cheered. "We're a hundred and thirty strong, led by a captain who, if nothing else, knows how to fight. I figure that every one of you, who at this very moment is richer than the wealthiest merchant you've ever known, will not so easily give up the treasure in our hold. Our fortunes are at stake . . . and so are our lives. So I ask you: Do you swear to fight to the death?"

"Aye, Captain!" the crew roared.

"Do you swear that no matter how dire the situation, you will never surrender?"

"Aye, Captain!"

"Then all is not lost, for we have the best fighting force on the sea! So let's give the English a beating they won't ever forget."

"Bravo, Malroux! Long live the captain!"

Scared yet eager, Louis braced for battle. At least this time, he would be fighting to save his riches rather than help a country too cheap to pay him any wages.

Malroux ordered the *Pearl* to engage the *Comet*, while the *Iphigénie* squared off against the *Trincomalee*. Then he strode up and down the deck, shouting encouraging words to his primed crew. In the fading light, Louis looked in the faces of his shipmates and saw a steely fierceness fired by greed, survival, and hatred for the English.

He loaded his musket and felt a strange sensation — he looked forward to combat. When the ships drew within range, they traded shots with cannons and muskets. The battle had begun. Yelling and screaming, Louis and the others fired from every vantage point, from yardarms, rigging, bow, and stern through the night and into the next day. Above the roar of the cannons, grenades, pistols, and muskets, he could hear the cries of distress of men who lay injured or dying.

Although he had been nicked and cut from flying debris, Louis hadn't been hurt until early afternoon when a sharp piece of wood from a grenade explosion sliced deep into his arm. Wincing in pain, Louis ducked behind a pile of rope and ripped off his bloody shirt. Gritting his teeth, he pulled the shard out of his flesh and tore off part of his shirt and wrapped it around his wound. Then he hustled over to Duncan toward the bow and began shooting again.

"Not as much fun as drinking rum, but, all in all, not a bad day for keeping your juices flowing, aye, lad?" said Duncan.

Before Louis could respond, another grenade exploded a

few feet away with such force it flung Louis against a railing, knocking him out. When he regained consciousness a few minutes later, he cleared his head and focused his eyes. Sprawled across from him was Duncan, bleeding badly from an open chest wound.

"Duncan!" Louis shouted. "Oh, no. Not you!"

"Lad, do . . . me . . . a . . . favor," Duncan sputtered between gasps. "Kill . . . more . . . English . . . for . . . me." Then he slumped over, dead.

There was no time to mourn. Filled with rage, Louis blasted away with his musket, trying his best to aim through his tear-filled eyes. The battle raged on for 14 hours, 16 hours, with neither side gaining an advantage.

But then, Louis and his shipmates found something that raised their spirits. Their cannons scored a direct hit on the *Trincomalee*'s mizzenmast (the rear mast), and it crashed forward over several of her guns, knocking them out of commission.

"The day is ours, lads!" shouted Malroux. "We'll see our port and we'll keep our gold!"

While chaos reigned on the *Trincomalee*, Malroux ordered his crew to unfurl the three topsails so they could make their escape. Despite the pain in his arm and the hurt in his heart, Louis found renewed energy as he manned a rope. *Let's get out of here and head for home!*

Suddenly, he heard a tremendous crack followed by shouts of alarm. He looked up and couldn't believe his eyes. The *Iphigénie's* foremast, weakened by several cannon shots, had snapped and was starting to fall. He dropped the rope and ran in the opposite direction as the huge mast crashed onto the deck and then rolled overboard, taking with it all her rigging and the hapless men who were aloft loosening the sails.

"This can't be happening to us," Louis moaned. He looked up on the poop deck where the captain was thrusting his fist in the air, screaming at his streak of bad luck.

Unable to escape, the *Iphigénie* was forced to continue fighting the *Trincomalee*. The *Pearl* couldn't help because she was undermanned and outgunned by the *Comet* and was forced to take evasive action so she wouldn't get boarded.

Although it was clear to everyone that the English had the upper hand, the crew of the *Iphigénie* refused to give up. In fact, they fought harder.

Darkness had fallen, but that did not stop the battle. The English scored several direct hits and so did the French guns. The *Trincomalee*'s main mast fell, blocking the line of fire of some of her guns, making the English ship unable to maneuver. Once again, the *Iphigénie* tried to flee, but because of her missing mast and lack of wind, she couldn't escape.

"There's only one way out!" Malroux shouted. "We must board her!"

Armed with his musket, a boarding ax, and a dagger in his waist, Louis stood on the railing as his ship came about and slammed into the side of the *Trincomalee*. With grenades raining down on the deck, the French privateers charged onto the enemy's ship. Twenty of the strongest seamen, wielding long lances, held the English at bay while the rest, laying down a murderous round of musket fire, made their assault. Like his crewmates, Louis was beyond pain, beyond exhaustion. He was fighting on instinct alone. For survival. For the treasure. Nothing could stop him.

In the deadly darkness, the determined Frenchmen slashed, shot, and stabbed their way from one end of the *Trincomalee* to the other until the retreating English took cover in their gun deck below. Just when it looked like the French could finally declare victory, shrieks from below froze everyone topside.

Louis looked down into the holes of a hatchway and saw an orange glow. "Fire!" he shouted. "The ship is on fire!"

Within seconds, flames shot up through the deck.

"Get back on the *Iphigénie* before this ship blows up!" ordered Malroux.

For the first time since the boarding, Louis felt a wave of panic. He fled in sheer terror and leaped back onto his own vessel. Seconds later, he was knocked off his feet by a thunderous explosion that shook the *Iphigénie* and covered her in a cloud of fire, ash, smoke, and debris. The blast had toppled her remaining two masts. When Louis staggered to his feet, he saw the blazing *Trincomalee* slowly sink into the inky water.

I can't believe I'm still alive, he thought. There was no time to count his blessings. The *Iphigénie* was listing to starboard and sinking.

Malroux shouted, "It won't be long before she founders. Get into the longboats!" The crewmen jumped in and rowed around the stricken vessel, plucking survivors out of the water. Louis cringed when he realized that they had left several badly wounded seamen aboard the sinking ship, but there was nothing anyone could do for them. *At least the sea will give them a swift death,* he thought.

The longboats rowed toward the *Pearl,* which along with the *Comet,* had ceased firing after the *Trincomalee* had exploded. Louis was near the stern of a longboat with 12 others, including Malroux. Shortly after they pushed off from the *Iphigénie,* the captain shouted, "I left my letter of marque in my cabin. Row back to the ship."

The sailors looked at one another warily because they knew if they came too close to the sinking ship, they could get sucked down with her, but they obeyed his orders. They rowed to a tangle of sails, ropes, and rigging floating next to the nearly submerged vessel. Malroux scrambled onto the deck and into his flooded cabin where he snatched his papers and slogged back to the longboat.

"Hurry, Captain. The ship is going down!" Louis yelled.

Malroux leaped toward the longboat but became entangled in the rigging and ropes. He struggled to free himself while sailors in the bow grabbed his arms and tried to pull him into the boat. But he was hopelessly snagged.

Within seconds, the *Iphigénie* let out a loud gurgle and slipped under the water, taking down with her the treasure, her captain, and the longboat of the men who had tried to save him. Louis and the others leaped into the sea but were pulled under by the current caused by the sinking ship.

Although Louis was slightly built, he was a strong swimmer. Clawing and kicking against the flow that was dragging him deeper under the black sea, Louis refused to give up. His lungs burning in pain and craving air, he finally freed himself from the grip of the current and burst to the surface, gagging and coughing.

He was soon fished out by mates on another longboat and brought aboard the *Pearl*. Meanwhile, the *Comet*'s crew had called it quits and sailed off.

The battle — which lasted 20 grueling hours — was finally over.

But it was terribly costly. Nearly 100 seamen aboard the *Iphigénie* and 115 British sailors went to a watery grave.

As the *Pearl* headed home, the dejected survivors silently performed their duties, talking only when necessary to run the ship. They were lost in their sorrowful private thoughts of what might have been. All they had to show for their efforts were the captured *Pearl* and 50 Arabian horses. The rest of the crew was full of heartache for the loss of their captain, crewmates, ship — and, of course, their treasure.

Well, at least I can say I was rich for a little while, thought Louis. *Too bad it was only for five days. Too bad I never got to spend any of it. I wonder, what's worse? To have great wealth and lose it, or not to have ever had it in the first place.* He shrugged. *I guess I should be thankful about the one thing I do have — my life.*

After the Iphigénie *disaster, Louis Garneray joined France's most famous privateer, Robert Surcouf, in 1800. Louis finally hit it rich at age 17 when the ship he was on captured a merchant vessel loaded with treasure. But in 1806, Louis was captured by the English and spent eight years on a prison ship in Portsmouth harbor where he sharpened his skills as a portrait painter. Released in 1814, Louis returned to France and spent the rest of his life as a well-known artist of naval scenes. This story is based on his memoirs,* Seaman Garneray: Voyages, Aventures et Combats, *which was first published in France in 1851.*

TAKING FRENCH LEAVE

CHARLES CRONEA, CABIN BOY FOR PRIVATEER JAMES CAMPBELL

Charles Cronea found his first few months aboard a French Navy ship hard and somewhat boring. But the 14-year-old apprentice seaman hoped it would lead to an adventurous life — at least more exciting than what he faced if he stayed at home in Marseilles, France.

Working as a cabin boy in 1819, he cleaned the captain's quarters, brought his food, and did other chores for him and the officers. The wiry, dark-haired youth got along well with everyone except Guy Monet, the 15-year-old know-it-all apprentice favored by the captain. Whenever he could, Guy would ridicule Charles. Typical was the day Guy sneered at him and scoffed, "Don't you even know how to make a proper knot?" Then, in front of some sailors, Guy showed off by retying the knots that Charles had done. "Boys from Marseilles have thumbs for fingers," Guy said to the chuckles of the sailors and the embarrassment of the cabin boy.

On a transatlantic voyage to New York, Charles decided to

get even. With a rope, he rigged a bucket of dirty mop water over a doorway and called to Guy, "I need your help." When Guy appeared, Charles yanked on the rope. But the knot wasn't tied the right way. Although the heavy wooden bucket tipped over and doused Guy just as Charles had intended, it also crashed on Guy's head. The impact knocked him out cold and opened up a nasty gash that required the attention of the surgeon onboard.

Captain Yves Saint-Pierre was outraged when he heard about Charles's prank. "Boy, front and center!" he ordered Charles. "This is the Navy of the French Republic, not a school play yard. You are a disgrace for playing a bad joke on a fellow seaman and for improperly tying your knots. You are going to learn how to tie knots correctly on a 'cat,' and then we will test them on your bare back."

"Sorry, sir. I don't understand."

"Oh, you will," the captain hissed. "You will."

Following Saint-Pierre's orders, the quartermaster (the second-in-charge) sat Charles down and showed him how to make a cat-o'-nine-tails — a thick stick with nine short knotted ropes tied to it. When Charles finished making it, he sensed what it was for, and became queasy.

Two sailors grabbed him and stripped off his shirt. He was spread-eagled on his stomach and tied to an iron grate on the deck. As the other seamen crowded around to watch, the quartermaster flogged the boy on his bare back 10 times with the cat-o'-nine-tails. With each stinging lash, Charles flinched, but he refused to utter a sound. *Don't cry out*, he told himself. *They want you to squeal.*

The pain was unbearable, and the flogging left his back

raw and bleeding. "Here, let me wash off the blood," said the quartermaster, pouring a bucket of saltwater on the open wounds. Never had Charles felt such sharp pain — like a thousand needles stabbing him in the back. And yet despite his slender build and young age, he remained tight-lipped.

That night as Charles lay on his stomach on his cot, a junior officer named Gustave Duval came over to him and said, "Lad, you held up like a tough seadog."

"I didn't deserve that flogging," Charles muttered. "Maybe a lash or two . . ."

"I agree. Saint-Pierre is a mean bucko. He's worse than some pirates."

"The first chance I get, I'm taking French leave."

"Hush, lad. You don't want anyone to know you plan on deserting the ship. Keep it to yourself." Duval winked and added, "You might get your opportunity soon."

About a week later, the ship docked in New York. That night, Duval woke up Charles and whispered, "Are you serious about deserting?" When Charles nodded, Duval said, "Then gather your things and come with me."

The boy grabbed his meager belongings in a canvas bag and sneaked off the ship with Duval. "Are you taking a French leave, too?" Charles asked.

"Aye, lad. Saint-Pierre is too vicious to serve under. I'm signing on with a ship from Baltimore. Wish to join me?"

"Sure!"

Within days, they were on the *Hotspur*, a sleek schooner equipped with six guns and designed to outsail most anything afloat. The 15 new crewmen met their new captain, James Campbell, who told them, "You are about enter the service of Jean Laffite of Campeachy. Under his leadership, we will engage in privateering cruises off the coast of Mexico in search of Spanish ships."

The men cheered.

"Lad," Duval said to Charles, "we'll soon be filling our pockets with gold doubloons. We're going after Spanish galleons [ships] loaded with treasure."

"Duval, what's a doubloon?"

"The largest of Spanish coins and worth about seven weeks' wages for an average seaman."

"Who is this man Laffite?"

"A clever and rich Frenchman operating out of Galveston, Texas. He commands dozens of privateers, and he also runs a thriving market in slaves and contraband, too. I tell you, Charles, we'll have so much money we'll each need our own boat to carry it all."

The *Hotspur* soon arrived at Jean Laffite's rickety pirate port of Campeachy, built near the entrance of Galveston Bay on Snake Island, named after the thousands of poisonous cottonmouths that inhabited the area.

Charles walked with Duval through the bustling but seedy town where about 1,000 sailors lived in hundreds of crudely built huts. Some had glass windows while most had only sailcloth covering the openings. Charles saw rough-looking seamen of different races and nationalities mending sails and fixing ropes while yakking in French, Spanish, Portuguese, and English. Their scraggly hair, scruffy beards, and weathered skin gave the appearance they were mean cutthroats. He noticed there were hardly any women. The place was dirty and smelly.

"I thought you said Laffite's pirates were rich," said Charles.

"This town was founded only two years ago, so it's not exactly Paris," Duval said. "You watch. When our ships return with all the booty we plan to seize, this town will be gleaming in gold. Mansions will spring up. The streets will be teeming with hand-carved carriages. It will be a paradise. And we will be bathing in doubloons."

At the edge of town, Charles and Duval watched as hundreds of slaves were taken off a vessel and forced into large wooden pens. "Most every ship of Laffite's returns to Campeachy with a load of Africans taken from captured Spanish slave ships," Duval explained. "I hear that Laffite sells them to plantation owners for about a dollar a pound. Can you imagine the huge profits he collects?"

"Is money all you think about, Duval?"

"Of course. What else is there?"

Back on board the *Hotspur*, Charles was made cabin boy for Captain Campbell, a stern but fair man who was quick to scold but ready to praise whenever warranted. The captain was a strict disciplinarian who expected everyone to do his job to the best of his ability. Occasionally, Campbell would snap at the boy because he was a step or two too late in delivering a map or hadn't cleaned the cabin to the captain's high standards. Still, Charles found conditions better on the *Hotspur* than on the French naval ship that he and Duval had deserted.

Campbell was Laffite's most trusted privateer, which made many of the other captains jealous, especially because he brought in the most booty. Unlike some captains who were more pirate than privateer, Campbell followed a strict code of attacking only Spanish ships and leaving vessels of other nationalities alone. He also did whatever he could to capture vessels without bloodshed. As long as they didn't put up a fight, he treated his Spanish captives with civility and put them ashore before scuttling their ship.

Shortly after the *Hotspur* sailed off in search of prey, Campbell named Duval his first mate. The Frenchman was now the captain's right-hand man, and the one who would take over command if anything happened to Campbell.

In addition to being a cabin boy, Charles also helped two salty gunners, "Crazy Ben" Dollivar and Jean-Baptiste Callistre. In charge of a brass six-pound cannon, the two had been in Laffite's service for nine years.

Dollivar, whose huge hooked nose towered over a full dark beard, projected an aura of fierceness.

"Why do they call you Crazy Ben?" Charles asked Dollivar.

"'Cause I am," he growled. "I was orphaned at a tender age and raised by my uncle on a plantation in Georgia. He was a cruel man who took a particular relish in flogging me most every day while I picked cotton from sun up to sun down. The strange thing was that at night he would read me the Bible by candlelight. When I was about your age, I ran away and went to sea."

He pointed to an ugly six-inch scar that extended from above his right eye to behind his right ear. "See this? It's from a saber in a fight with a sailor who called me crazy. I wasn't then, but after getting sliced like this, I turned a little crazy."

Callistre chuckled. "Aye, mate. You're a loon. But then you have to be if you love guns the way you do."

"And you don't, Callistre? You sleep with them."

Callistre, who sported a thin mustache and brown hair pulled back in a ponytail, was a French-born sailor in his thirties whose wife and two children lived in the bayous of Louisiana. He asked Charles, "Tell me, my young Frenchman, do you love guns? The sound of deafening discharges? The smell of gunpowder? The enjoyment of watching a cannonball crash onto the deck of the enemy?"

Charles shrugged. "I've never been around them much."

"You will now. You're our powder monkey — our assistant in times of battle. Your job is to carry buckets of powder from the ship's magazine to the guns."

Callistre turned to Dollivar and asked, "Crazy Ben, do you think our babe-in-arms here will make a good powder monkey?"

"If not, we'll just throw him overboard," replied Dollivar matter-of-factly.

The boy didn't know if Dollivar was serious, but decided he wouldn't give either gunner a reason to toss him in the drink.

Less than a week out of Campeachy, the *Hotspur* encountered her first Spanish vessel, a schooner with four guns that tried to outrun the privateers. Dollivar and Callistre fired a shot over her bow as a signal to heave-to for boarding. The vessel wouldn't stop.

"Looks like we're in for a little fight," said Dollivar. "Let's convince them that's a mistake."

As Charles raced back and forth, lugging buckets of powder, the gunners fired round after round into the Spanish vessel, tearing away rigging and sails and weakening her foremast. The *Hotspur* closed in for the kill when the Spanish ship sent up a white flag of surrender. Charles heard the crew aboard the stricken vessel yelling frantically in Spanish.

"The lily livers now want us to stop shooting at them," crowed Callistre.

"I guess we made our point. But let's keep firing on them. It's so much fun," said Dollivar.

But the gunners stopped when Campbell ordered a ceasefire. Moments later, he sent a longboat with an armed crew led by Duval to take over command of the Spanish ship. The privateers carefully searched belowdecks and forced the enemy captain at the point of a sword into revealing where his treasure was hidden onboard.

With the ships side by side, Duval yelled out to the *Hotspur* crew, "It's a great prize! Gold bars, coins, and silver plate!" The seamen erupted in cheers. But none looked as crazed or as jubilant as Duval.

After the treasure, gunpowder, and supplies were brought aboard the *Hotspur* along with the Spanish crew, Campbell ordered the vessel set on fire. To the moans of the captives, the ship burst into flames and then sank in the gulf.

True to his word, Campbell sailed to a spot on the Mexican coast and released the Spaniards before heading off to his next conquest.

For the next eight months, Campbell's swift vessel captured one Spanish prize after another, making off with bars of gold and silver (known as bullion), coins, supplies, gunpowder, and tobacco, which was always in demand. When the *Hotspur*'s belly was full of booty from the capture of eight ships, Campbell delivered every bit of it to Laffite in Campeachy. The crew got its share, with the bulk going to Laffite.

Shortly after returning to the sea in the fall of 1820, the privateers plundered another Spanish ship of gold, silver, and rum. That night, Charles saw Duval on the forecastle, talking softly to 10 Frenchmen who were part of the *Hotspur*'s crew. The only Frenchmen not in the group were Callistre and the cabin boy.

Charles eavesdropped without them knowing it. Whispering in French, Duval told the others, "Why should we turn all this booty over to Laffite? Why should we do all the work and get only a tiny portion of the riches? We can keep it all for ourselves if we seize control of the ship. Later tonight, when we're on watch, we'll kill Campbell and any seaman who won't join us. Just think. The more we kill, the less we have to share."

A mutiny! Charles thought. *I've got to alert the captain.* He slipped belowdecks and burst into Campbell's cabin.

"What is the meaning of coming in here unannounced?" thundered Campbell.

"Forgive me, sir, but this is mighty important." Charles blurted out Duval's plans for the murderous takeover of the *Hotspur.*

Campbell rounded up the remainder of the crew who were loyal to him. He emerged on deck and told everyone, "We should celebrate tonight over our latest prize. Charles, break out the rum!"

The men cheered as Charles ran around filling the men's cups. The loyal crewmen pretended to drink but really didn't, while the French guzzled the rum until they were so drunk they fell asleep. When they woke up hours later, their hands and feet were bound.

Duval protested and claimed any talk of a mutiny was all a misunderstanding. Then his eyes grew big and he pointed to Charles. "You! You were spying on us, you traitor!"

"Gag them," Campbell ordered. The crew tied rags in the mouths of the conspirators. Two days later, the captain dropped the 10 Frenchmen off on a deserted island and gave them a cask of water and food for a week. "You are a disgrace and don't deserve my mercy!" he shouted at them. "But I give it to you with the hope that you rot on this godforsaken island!"

Campbell didn't seem the same after he thwarted the mutiny. He became moody and irritable for weeks, and remained upset that despite his fair treatment of the crew, 10 were willing to kill him to enrich themselves. At one point, Charles overheard the captain mutter to an officer, "I never should have made Duval my first mate. Never trust a Frenchman."

Charles was receiving the brunt of the captain's anger. The boy could never do anything right anymore no matter how hard he tried. Once again, it was a bucket of water that brought him a punishment that he didn't deserve.

While carrying a full pail on deck, Charles tripped and spilled water over Campbell's shoes. It didn't seem a big deal to the cabin boy, but the captain was enraged. He grabbed Charles by the ears and thundered, "You clumsy idiot! Haven't you learned how to carry a simple bucket of water?"

"Sorry, sir, it was an accident. It won't happen again."

Still yanking on the boy's ears, the captain snarled, "You need time to think about being more careful, you bottlehead." He dragged Charles to the nearest cannon and ordered, "Stand on that gun and don't move until I tell you. If you fall off, I'll make you stand on it the rest of the day."

Sailors gathered around as the barefoot cabin boy climbed on the iron cannon. It wasn't easy to stand on the gun barrel and hold his balance, because the ship was sailing. For the next half hour, Charles struggled to keep from falling by leaning and swaying as the ship rolled in the gentle swells. *This is the thanks I get for warning him about the mutiny,* he thought. *Maybe I should have let the others take over the ship. The man is crazy and obviously hates all Frenchmen. I can't take this anymore. As soon as we get back to port, I'm getting off for good.* Hearing the chortles from crewmen, he felt as humiliated as he was angry. He noticed the only seaman who didn't find the punishment funny was Callistre.

After a half hour, the captain shouted to Charles, "Get off that gun. Let that be a lesson for you, Cronea. I will not tolerate any incompetence on the *Hotspur*! Now go about your tasks — and do them without any more bungling."

That night, Charles complained bitterly to Callistre about how unfairly the captain had treated him. "I want off of this ship. He has treated me like scum for no good reason. He hates me because I'm French."

"Aye, mate. I fear you might be right. He's been snapping at me without cause ever since the mutiny attempt. I think it's time to say *au revoir* to the *Hotspur* soon. It's been too long since I've last seen my family on Bayou Teche. My pockets are full of doubloons, and it's time I spend them on my loved ones."

About a month later, in November 1820, the two saw their chance to leave. The *Hotspur* was loaded with the plunder from six ships that she had captured during the previous weeks. While sailing near the mouth of the Mermentau River in southwest Louisiana for fresh water, she ran aground.

Waves from a storm battered the stuck ship, and she began to break apart. The crew frantically tried to salvage the booty, but they were no match for the churning water, and most of their treasure was lost. The seamen rowed to shore to save their lives. Rather than trek west with the others to Campeachy, Charles and Callistre headed north into the Louisiana bayous.

During their walk, Callistre laughed and said, "Charles, remember what Campbell said when he forced you to stand on the cannon? 'I will not tolerate any incompetence on the *Hotspur*!' And then what does he do? He runs his own ship aground and watches her sink and loses all the booty."

Callistre returned to his family in St. Martinsville while Charles settled in Abbeville 25 miles away. A year later, the teenager and the veteran seaman discovered that they missed the life of privateering. They headed to Campeachy, planning to serve under one of Laffite's other captains.

When the two arrived at the pirate port, they were shocked. Every house, hut, slave pen, and corral had been burned; even the docks were destroyed. Nothing was left but charred rubble and snakes. The harbor was empty.

They sought out Dollivar, who lived nearby, for an explanation. "A few months after we lost the *Hotspur*, a warship from the U.S. Navy anchored offshore," he said. "The captain, Lieutenant Kearney, had orders to evict all the pirates from Campeachy. The orders came directly from the president of the United States, James Monroe, and Kearney personally delivered them to Laffite. It was odd because the two were friendly toward each other. Kearney said that too many of Laffite's captains were raiding American ships, and that the federal government was determined to put an end to this piracy. Laffite had to stop his operation and destroy Campeachy, or the navy would do it for him. He knew he couldn't win if it turned into a war. This past spring, we carted off everything of value and burned the entire town he had created. It's all over, mates."

Callistre nodded sadly. "You're right, Crazy Ben. It's time for this old seadog to give up the sea." Turning to Charles, he asked, "What about you?"

"I'll think of something," Charles replied. "I don't know what, but I'll make sure whatever I do next won't involve a water bucket."

Charles eventually married and moved to the Galveston, Texas, area where he fought for Texas in its war of independence against Mexico. After Texas won, he remained there and raised watermelons. Callistre returned to his family in Louisiana while Dollivar stayed in the Galveston area and lived a simple life, paying for his expenses from the money he earned as a privateer.

Captain Campbell and his wife, Mary, settled north of

Galveston and raised cattle on a small farm. He seldom talked openly about his days as a privateer.

Laffite left Campeachy, but his fate is not known. Some reports say he captained a pirate ship in the waters off South America. He supposedly died from injuries he received during a sea battle off the coast of Venezuela in 1822.

"DEAD CATS DON'T MEW"

NICKOLA COSTA, CABIN BOY FOR PIRATE DON PEDRO GIBERT

Cabin boy Nickola Costa was all ears while clearing the table in the captain's quarters. The conversation between Don Pedro Gibert and trusted mate Francisco Ruiz jangled Nickola's nerves.

"I tell you, Captain, we can take her easily," Ruiz said. "We've got the guns, the speed, and the manpower. We board her, rob her, and scuttle her. Slick as the sweat off my brow."

"Then what are we waiting for, Ruiz?" said the captain. "Let's take it to the crew, and if they agree we'll chase her down."

Nickola's heart started beating faster. *What?* thought Nickola. *We're a merchant ship and now we're going to turn pirate?* Shaken by the thought, he fumbled a dish but caught it before it struck the floor. Then he hurried out of the room. *Me on a pirate ship?*

The idea of robbing the rich had a wicked thrill to it because he was poor and hardly an innocent 15-year-old. In his native Brazil, he had his share of fistfights and engaged in petty theft.

And he knew when he joined the crew of the schooner *Panda* the previous year that Captain Gibert was a shady character, a known smuggler along the Florida and Cuban coasts. In fact, rumor had it that the cargo in the ship's hold — gunpowder and muskets — had been stolen from a Spanish fort by pirates and sold at a huge discount to Gibert, who planned to trade the arms in Africa.

Smuggling and dealing in stolen goods were far different than piracy. As exciting as it sounded to Nickola, he had misgivings. It was the summer of 1832, and piracy was almost a thing of the past in the Caribbean. He knew what happened to sea rovers who were caught by the authorities — they ended up at the end of a hangman's noose. He shuddered when he imagined a rope tightening around his neck.

He went on deck to hear the captain address the crew of 40 Portuguese-speaking sailors. Tall and muscular, Gibert had a commanding presence. When he spoke in his rich, baritone voice, his round head bobbed, causing the waves in his long jet-black hair to bounce. His inky eyes grew large, and his pearl white teeth flashed when he spoke.

"My officers and I want to attack the merchant ship off our port bow about three miles away." The crew began to murmur. "What do you say?" Gibert asked them. "Are you with me?" Most of the men shouted, "Aye!" Nickola gave a halfhearted cheer and noticed that the cook and three seamen kept quiet.

"If there's a man here who doesn't wish to participate in this venture, then let him speak now," the captain told the crew. "You will be free to leave this ship at the next port, but be denied any share of the booty. You have thirty seconds to decide. But make no mistake. Unless you speak up now, I expect each to give his all."

Gibert held up his gold pocket watch for half a minute. No one said a word. "Well, then," he said, "let us see what spoils are aboard that ship."

On board the *Panda* — a fast, sleek schooner painted black with a white stripe — the men snapped to Gibert's orders as they prepared for their first attempt at piracy. In the center of the ship was a long brass cannon fixed on a carriage that revolved in a circle. On each side of the deck were mounted guns of smaller caliber.

Nickola, who wore a yellow knit cap over his long brown hair, was a stocky teenager whose chestnut-colored eyes were always darting, trying to see everything that was happening. Now as a pirate, his job was to make sure the gunners had plenty of gunpowder if a sea battle broke out.

"Costa," said Ruiz. "If they speak English and don't understand Portuguese, you'll have to translate."

Nickola nodded. He was the only one on board who knew some English.

Ruiz then handed Nickola a dagger. "You might need this — just in case."

Nickola gulped and took the dagger from him quickly so Ruiz wouldn't see the youth's trembling hand. *I guess I'm turning pirate.*

An hour later, the *Panda* closed in on the merchant ship and fired two shots off her bow, forcing the ship to surrender. When the *Panda* came alongside it, Gibert called out to her captain. No one on the other vessel spoke Portuguese, so Nickola had to act as a translator. "What is your name and what are you carrying?" he asked the captain.

"I am John Butman, captain of the *Mexican*. We sailed out of Boston and are bound for Rio de Janeiro, Brazil. We are carrying tea and also potassium nitrate for making fertilizer. And who are you?"

Nickola whispered to Gibert what Butman had said. Repeating Gibert's words in English, Nickola told Butman, "It does not matter who we are. We are coming aboard, so don't anyone move."

Sixteen men, including Nickola, Gibert, and Ruiz, armed with knives and pistols, rowed over to the *Mexican* and boarded her.

"What is it you want?" asked Butman.

Translating for Gibert, Nickola said, "We believe you are carrying money. Give it to us now, or we will cut your throats."

Butman shook his head. "We have no money."

Gilbert didn't wait for the translation. He gripped Butman by the arm, twisted it behind his back, and put a cutlass to his neck.

"My captain says he will kill you and a crewman every minute until someone tells the truth," Nickola said.

"You win!" squealed the captain. "I'll show you where the money is." He led the pirates down into his quarters, where he lifted up two loose floorboards, revealing 10 wooden boxes. Inside each box was two thousand dollars' worth of silver.

"Ho-ho!" shouted Gibert triumphantly. "We struck it rich!"

Nickola had never seen so much money in his life. He caught himself breathing rapidly from sheer excitement. *Being a pirate is pretty good*, he thought. *We scare wealthy people, steal their money, and nobody gets hurt.*

Gibert ordered the *Mexican*'s crew to carry the silver to his rowboat, which then transferred the booty over to the *Panda*. The captured sailors were then shoved into the forecastle of the *Mexican* while the pirates ransacked the cabin, opened all the crew's chests and trunks, and helped themselves to new clothes, tobacco, and knives. Next, they rifled through the sailors' pockets, taking watches, coins, and rings.

Translating Gibert's words, Nickola told the captives, "Finding hidden money is like seeing a rat. There's always more than you think."

"I swear you have taken all we have," Butman declared.

The pirates continued their search anyway, even emptying the pickle barrel and water barrels for concealed valuables. But there was nothing left to steal. After all the booty had been collected, Ruiz pointed to the captives and asked Gibert, "What should we do with them, Captain?"

"Dead cats don't mew," replied Gibert, who then went back aboard the *Panda*.

Nickola was stunned by the captain's orders. *Kill them? But why? We've stolen everything. They didn't put up a fight. Why should we kill them? I can't watch this.*

Nickola started walking to the opposite end of the *Mexican* when Ruiz grabbed his arm and said, "Costa. Come here and help us." Pointing to the hold where the captives were now confined, he said, "Fasten every hatch and lock every companionway so they can't escape."

"What then?"

"Help us scuttle the boat."

While Nickola secured the latches, the other pirates were destroying the *Mexican*. They cut rigging, including the tiller ropes so she couldn't steer; slashed sails into ribbons; cut loose spars; smashed the ship's instruments, including the compasses; and toppled the yardarms.

"Costa, help me roll this barrel of tar into the cook's galley," Ruiz ordered.

"What for?"

"To use it to set the ship on fire."

Nickola wanted to shout, *Are you crazy, Ruiz? These sailors don't deserve to die — and certainly not by fire. We'll be more than pirates. We'll be murderers.* But he didn't say that out of fear that he would be considered a coward — or worse, he would be thrown into the hold with the captives and burned alive.

As the pirates piled up tarred rope yarn and other combustibles into the cook's galley, Nickola knew he had to save the captives' lives, or at least give them a chance to escape. He lifted up one of the hatches and looked down at 13 pairs of eyes.

One of the crewmen, who understood some Portuguese, shouted to him, "I heard what you're going to do to us. Have you no soul? No humanity?"

"Hush," said Nickola. "I'm going to leave this hatch unlocked. As soon as we leave, you can escape, hopefully in time to put out the fire."

From behind him, Nickola heard Ruiz, "Costa! What are you doing?"

"Uh, making sure the hatch is fastened tight."

"Let's go. We've torched the ship."

As Nickola ran across the deck, he noticed that the pirates had dismantled the mainsail and tossed it on top of the galley so it would quickly catch fire and burn the ship faster. *I hope those poor sailors get out of there in time*, he thought.

When the pirates returned to the *Panda*, they danced in celebration over their plunder. But Nickola remained at the stern, peering at the smoke pouring out from the *Mexican*. He thought, *I hope they survive.* He watched the smoke until he could no longer see the burning ship on the horizon.

Over the next few months, the *Panda* was engaged in smuggling guns between Cuba and southern Florida. No one knew the fate of the *Mexican*, and no one seemed to care except for Nickola, the African cook, and the three crewmen who didn't participate.

In the fall of 1833, the *Panda* reached Cape Lopez, near the equator on the West African coast. The ship anchored a mile up the Nazareth River outside a tiny hut village headed by a native who called himself King Gula. Gibert traded the king cloth and guns for tortoise shells, ivory, palm oil, and gum. The captain also gave the king silver trinkets as gifts. In return, the king provided the crew with food and friendship.

Two weeks later, Nickola and two dozen crewmen came down with high fevers and cramps from a contagious disease that had struck the village. Hoping to prevent the illness from spreading further, Gibert took all his men and sailed about 250 miles west in the Gulf of Guinea to Prince's Island so they could recover. The island was a gathering place for pirates, smugglers, and slavers.

When Nickola recovered, he went ashore where he struck up a conversation with a British smuggler named Kent, who told him, "You say you're from the *Panda*? The navy is looking for you blokes."

"What do you mean?"

"I heard you plundered an American vessel, locked everyone belowdecks, and set her on fire. Only they escaped. They returned home and reported what happened. The American government sent a cruiser to the African coast and searched for you for months. Only they didn't find you. But they told the Royal Navy to keep an eye out for you, and if they find you, to take you into custody."

Nickola put his hands to his head. *I tried to help them and now thanks to me, we might get captured. Maybe I should have let them die. "Dead cats don't mew." But I couldn't do that. It would have been murder. But then, what difference does it make? If we're caught and found guilty, they'll hang us anyway.*

Nickola didn't want to hear any more. He broke off the conversation and rushed back to the *Panda* and told Captain Gibert the news. At first, Gibert didn't believe him. But after he and Ruiz spoke directly to several smugglers on the island, they learned it was true. The *Panda* left Prince's Island immediately and returned to the village on the Nazareth River, seeking the protection of King Gula and his warriors.

Several days later, word reached Gibert that the British warship *Curlew*, captained by Lieutenant Henry Trotter, had arrived at Cape Lopez. It was only a matter of time before Trotter would try to capture them. Gibert commanded his crew to pile cotton and gunpowder in the cook's galley of the *Panda* so that if the British boarded the ship, the pirates would blow her up, killing their pursuers.

The following day, while acting as a lookout, Nickola shouted, "I see them! Three small boats are heading our way! I count about forty men!"

"Abandon ship!" Gibert ordered.

Ruiz rushed into the galley, lit a fuse, and jumped into the last rowboat and raced to shore with the others. The pirates hid in the woods and waited for the *Panda* to explode. But there was no blast when the British boarded her.

"Drat," said Ruiz. "The fuse must have died out. What bum luck."

From the *Panda*, the British began shooting at the pirates who returned the fire from behind trees along the shore. For Nickola, it was the first time he had fired a musket at another human being. He no longer considered the morality of trying to kill someone. There was no debate in his mind. *Someone is shooting at me so I'm shooting at him,* he told himself.

During the lengthy gun battle, a spark from a ricocheting bullet ignited the gunpowder in the cook's galley of the *Panda*, causing an enormous explosion that killed 5 British sailors and injured 10 others. The British retreated in their boats and returned to Cape Lopez. The *Panda* was destroyed.

Meanwhile, the pirates regrouped at the native village and prepared for another battle. With the help of King Gula and the promise of getting them more guns, Gibert rounded up about 100 warriors to join in the next fight against the British. Two weeks later, a native spy reported the British were heading upriver in two small boats with cannons and 30 armed men.

The musket-carrying pirates and the spear-wielding natives ran to a bend in the river, climbed into their canoes, and charged the British. To Nickola, this battle was much scarier because there was little cover in the canoe that he shared with Ruiz, two fellow pirates, and two natives. Fearing for his life, he crouched as low as he could while paddling. Like the others, he was shouting curses and yelling war cries to intimidate the British. For the cabin boy, his screaming helped hide his fear.

The well-armed British fired their small cannons and scored direct hits that sank several canoes. A volley of gunshots struck the natives in the lead boats, wiping them out. Seeing their fellow warriors killed, the rest of the natives quit fighting. Some paddled to shore; others jumped overboard and swam off.

By now, several of the pirates had turned around, reached the shore, and disappeared into the woods. Unfortunately for Nickola, his canoe wasn't one of them. Ruiz and the others kept firing until they ran out of ammunition.

When the battle was over, the British had captured Nickola, Ruiz, Gibert, and nine others. The prisoners were put in irons, taken to England, and then transferred to Boston to stand trial. During the long, demanding months of confinement aboard the ships, Nickola kept wondering how he ended up like this. He was just a cabin boy looking for a little adventure; now he was a captured pirate who faced a possible death sentence.

On the voyage to Boston, Nickola made up his mind that he wouldn't mention that he had unlocked the hatch so the crew of the *Mexican* could escape. He reasoned that if the truth was known and he was acquitted (found innocent), he would be murdered by another pirate for being a traitor. If he was convicted, he would probably hang anyway. *I will act with defiance in court,* he told himself. *I will scoff and laugh and pretend I'm not interested. I need to convince the others that I'm as bad a pirate as they are. It's because of me that we're in this awful spot.*

On November 11, 1834 — more than two years after the attack of the *Mexican* — 12 men from the *Panda* were officially charged with piracy in the U.S. Circuit Court. The thirteenth pirate died in his jail cell before his case was heard.

On the first day of the trial, the district attorney told the jury, "This is a solemn and an unusual scene. Here are twelve men, strangers to our country, indicted for a horrible offense, and now before you they face life or death. They are indicted for a daring crime, a flagrant violation of the laws, not only of the United States but of every other civilized people."

Members of the *Mexican* then testified about that fateful day. They recalled how they were threatened and beaten and left to burn alive. But then one of the pirates — they didn't know who — unlocked one of the hatches so they could escape.

First mate Thomas Fuller testified, "After the pirates left, we climbed out of the hatch and ran onto the deck, which was on fire. We managed to get it under control and decided to let it smolder. We were afraid that if we put it out, the pirates would know that we had escaped, and they would come back. We let it smoke so the pirates would be convinced the ship would burn and sink, taking everyone down.

"The ship was badly damaged, what with the sails, rope, and rigging cut. We mended the sails and repaired the yardarms and spars until we got the *Mexican* sailing again. Captain Butman was a shrewd one, he was. Before the pirates boarded, he hid a spare compass, quadrant, sexton, and other important instruments under a pile of old ropes. Lucky for us, the pirates never found them. We headed straight home and told authorities of this vicious attack."

Because the evidence against the pirates was overwhelming, the pirate's attorney, George Hillard, tried to put the blame on Gibert and Ruiz, claiming the others were merely following orders.

When he argued on behalf of Nickola, Hillard said, "As for Costa, the cabin boy, only fifteen years old when the crime was committed. Should he die? Should the sword fall upon his neck? Some of you have children of your own. Suppose the news had reached you that your son was under trial for his life in a foreign country. Suppose you had been told that he faced execution because his captain and his officers had violated laws of a distant land. How would you feel?"

Not helping his cause any, Nickola shrugged and gazed around the courtroom as if he could care less that his attorney was trying to save his life. *I've got to act tough.*

During closing arguments, Hillard told the jury, "If you agree with me that the crew were mere servants of the captain, you cannot convict them. But if you do not agree with me, then I must address a few words to you in the way of mercy. It does not seem to me that the good of society requires the death of all these men. Do not let the sword of the law drip with the blood of vengeance."

The jury left to consider the fate of the defendants. The next morning, the pirates returned to the courthouse to hear the verdicts. Each prisoner was ordered to stand and hear his fate. The first was Captain Gibert.

"Jurors, look upon the prisoner," said the court clerk. "Prisoner, look upon the jurors. How say you, gentlemen of the jury? Is the prisoner at the bar, Don Pedro Gibert, guilty or not guilty?"

The foreman cleared his throat and said, "Guilty." Gibert didn't need a translator to understand. Without changing his expression, the captain nodded, then bowed slightly to the jury and sat down.

The same guilty verdict was pronounced against Ruiz and five more pirates. With each guilty verdict, Nickola shook his head and dug his fingers into the arms of his chair. *This keeps getting worse*, he thought. *They're going to convict all of us. We're all going to hang.* Still, he kept flashing ill-mannered gestures and sarcastic smiles.

But then his hopes rose when the foreman announced "Not guilty" for the cook and the three seamen who had remained on the *Panda* during the attack of the *Mexican.*

Now it was Nickola's turn. He stood up when his name was called. He had never been more scared — not even when the British were firing at him. To mask his nerves, he scowled and glared at the judge and jury.

The court clerk asked the jury foreman, "Is the prisoner at the bar, Nickola Costa, guilty or not guilty?"

"Not guilty."

Not guilty! Not guilty! Nickola repeated the words in his

mind. *Whew! Not guilty!* But outwardly, in what he considered a show of respect for those who were found guilty, he sneered and chuckled in scorn at the court.

And so the long ordeal was over for Nickola Costa, cabin boy. He was free to go his own way. Where he went, history doesn't say. After he walked out of the courthouse, he was never heard from again.

In the summer of 1835, the seven convicted pirates were hanged — the last men executed in the United States for piracy on the high seas.

This story is based in part on official statements from two Mexican crewmen and on The Pirates Own Book, *a collection of newspaper accounts, court records, and memoirs. The book, compiled by Charles Ellms, of Boston, was published in 1837, two years after the hangings.*

ABOUT THE AUTHOR

Allan Zullo is the author of more than 90 nonfiction books on subjects ranging from sports and the supernatural to history and animals.

He has written the bestselling Haunted Kids series, published by Scholastic, which are filled with chilling stories based on, or inspired by, documented cases from the files of ghost hunters. Allan has also introduced Scholastic readers to the Ten True Tales series, about kids who have met the challenges of dangerous, sometimes life-threatening, situations. In addition, he has authored two books about the real-life experiences of kids during the Holocaust — *Survivors: True Stories of Children in the Holocaust* and *Heroes of the Holocaust: True Stories of Rescues by Teens.*

Allan, the grandfather of three boys and the father of two grown daughters, lives with his wife on the side of a mountain near Asheville, North Carolina. To learn more about the author, visit his Web site at www.allanzullo.com.